THROWN A CURVE

a novel

SARA GRIFFITHS

THROWN A CURVE

a novel

SARA GRIFFITHS

bancroft
press

Published by Bancroft Press ("Books that enlighten")
P.O. Box 65360, Baltimore, MD 21209
800-637-7377
410-764-1967 (fax)
www.bancroftpress.com

Cover and interior design: Tammy Sneath Grimes, Crescent Communications
www.tsgcrescent.com • 814.941.7447

Author photo:

ISBN 1-890862-48-7
LCCN 2006938837

Printed in the United States of America

First Edition

1 3 5 7 9 10 8 6 4 2

To Jamie and Ben

CHAPTER 1

I sat alone in the high school principal's small office, waiting for my punishment. I leaned my elbows on the desk and covered my face with my hands. Why had I done it? What had I been thinking? How had I gotten to this low point in my life? I was a juvenile delinquent at age fourteen.

I'd never done anything wrong before. This was the first time I'd ever been inside a school principal's office. It was all my dad's fault. If he didn't hate me, if he hadn't said what he'd said, I wouldn't be here. I sighed and tried to remember better days, when my life was just about playing games, like baseball . . .

When I was seven years old, my father had bought season tickets to the Yankees' home baseball games. Having lived in New York his whole life, he was a loyal fan. He purchased two seats for each game. One ticket was always for himself, and the other ticket rotated between my two brothers. Brian was four years older than me, and Danny four years younger. Dad never put me in the rotation, and I never asked him to. I thought it was just a father-son thing.

When my brothers tried out for Little League that year, I sat in the bleachers, eating handfuls of Swedish fish, stretching their little bodies as far as I could before gulping them down. I watched the other fathers, looking thrilled and hopeful, cheering on their sons. My dad encouraged my brothers, but he looked even more intense than the other fathers.

After several hours of watching my brothers try out, I wandered onto the playground, took a few rides down the slide, and considered joining some of my classmates in a round of Double Dutch. But then one of the Little Leaguers hit a ball out of the park. It flew toward the playground, hit the ground, and rolled to a stop in front of me. I stared at the baseball's stitches. Its strange pattern put me in a trance that seemed to last for days. I'd never really thrown a baseball.

"Throw it back!" a coach yelled to me.

I picked up the ball and hurled it with all my might. It sailed over the fence, over the coach, over second base, and hit the pitcher in the head. Oops. I ran back to the playground, hoping no one had seen me.

On the ride home, I sat on the hump in the car's backseat, squished between Brian and Danny. I kept thinking about throwing that baseball. I wondered if I could be as good as my brothers.

"You boys did a good job out there today," my dad said to them. "Let's go out for ice cream."

As we were downing our sundaes at the ice cream parlor, my younger brother Danny said, "You can throw real good, Taylor. Daddy said so."

Back then, I thought my father knew everything. If he'd seen me throw that ball and thought it was good, then he was right. He was always right. But if I was good, why hadn't he told me so himself?

Later that night, I sat by my dad's feet as he napped on the couch and watched Tom Brokaw talk about the news in the Middle East.

"Hey, Dad?" I said.

"What?"

"I think I'll play baseball this summer, too."

Looking confused, he said nothing. He hadn't said much since my mother left us. And that had been two years ago.

Only one Little League team had been willing to take a seven-year-old girl—the Hawks. Their assistant coach was the nurse at my elementary school, and I only made the team because she'd gone on and on with the head coach about women's rights and other stuff I really hadn't understood. She promised to look out for me. Back then, I wasn't aware anyone needed to "look out for me."

I wanted to be a pitcher because Dad said I had a good arm. But the coaches put me in center field.

"You can make the throw to home, and you're too wild on the mound," Ms. Miller said.

I had a good summer playing with the Hawks. I loved playing baseball. When I was out there on the field, I was so happy.

It was weird how something so simple could make me feel so good.

The boys on the team hadn't cared I was a girl, but the parents had. They made comments to my father when he would pick me up after games. He just waved, nodded, and blew smoke rings from his cigar.

Dad never saw any of my games because Brian's games were always at the same time on Field Seven. My brother Brian was an excellent baseball player—his batting average was .297.

I thought I could've played better baseball if my dad had come to watch me. I wished he would sit in *my* stands, even once. I always looked for him, and when he wasn't there, it was hard not to cry. I kept thinking he'd come one day—maybe if I became a really good pitcher, never let any batters on base, and won the championship for my Little League team. He'd come, I figured, when I got really good.

With this in mind, I practiced every chance I got. Once, I pitched to Brian in the empty lot behind our house. He whiffed at three of my pitches in a row.

"You throw too high, Taylor!" Brian screamed.

He swung at them, I thought to myself. But he was eleven, and I was only seven, so I guessed he was right. Dad watched from the back porch, not saying anything. He just looked down, turned, and walked back into the house.

The next three summers, my dad sent me to my Aunt Maria's house in Cape May, New Jersey to help out with her bed and breakfast. Aunt Maria, my dad's sister, was widowed, and the only thing she knew about baseball was that the Little League field in town was too far away, and she didn't have time to drive me there. She wanted me to take dance lessons at the nearby studio, but I hung around the beach instead.

I hadn't understood why my dad would send me away during the summer baseball season. My one hope was playing fall ball when I got home. I missed playing summer Little League and being home with my brothers and my dad, but I figured my aunt did need a hand.

Some nights at Cape May, I played wiffleball on the beach with different kids who were on vacation. One day, I'd seen a family playing a game with real bats and balls. I was excited when I noticed they had gloves and bases, too, and even a makeshift pitcher's mound.

"Do you need an extra player?" I asked, eager to partici-pate.

"Sure, you can play outfield," said the man, who I assumed was the dad.

"Ugh. Outfield. What else is new?" I mumbled under my breath, frowning.

"Unless you want to be the pitcher," he said, sens-ing my disappointment at being directed to the outfield.

Darn right I wanted to be the pitcher. No one got a hit the first inning, or the second. By the third inning, the twins in the outfield sat down. By the end of the fourth inning, I again was asked to play outfield.

That had been the summer before I entered fifth grade. It was also before I realized my dad hated me.

After my first day as a fifth grader, I came home and headed toward my dad's office. I was going to tell him about my boring day and ask him to drive me to fall baseball practice. I heard him on the phone, so I stopped outside the door and listened. That's when I had heard it—the thing I should never have heard.

"Yeah, Charlie, uh-huh," he said. "It's just so embarrassing . . . having my daughter on the team instead of Brian . . . I'm the laughing stock of the office. The wrong kid got the right gift."

I stood frozen in the doorway. I didn't hear anything my dad said after that. Why would he have said that? *The wrong kid?* Why wasn't I the *right* kid? I felt my whole world come crashing down on me. I was like a building imploding on itself—so my life consisted only of dust and wreckage. That day, I decided to stop playing baseball, if that was the way my father really felt about me. I stopped believing everything my father said. More importantly, I think I stopped believing in anything.

CHAPTER 2

There comes a day in all kids' lives when they suddenly start seeing the bad things in the world—the evil that has been lurking around them. That day for me was when I heard my father say *those* words. After that, my whole attitude changed. It felt like dark clouds permanently loomed over my head, following me wherever I went. I lost interest in baseball, in talking to people, and in getting up early to see the morning sunshine. I became a sunglass-wearing, drag-me-out-of-bed kind of girl. I wanted to fade into the walls of my bedroom, never to be heard from again. I figured my whole life until then had been a lie. And the truth hurt.

School was the worst. Girls made me nervous because they'd formed cliques by the time we were in middle school, and I hadn't fit into any of them. I wasn't smart, but I wasn't dumb. I didn't wear makeup or tight clothes, but I didn't dress like a rebellious ghoul, either. I was somewhere in the middle, which to me felt like somewhere on the outside. I was removed from the field and forced to sit in the nosebleed seats—a spectator in my own life. Where was the clique for girls whose fathers hated them? Or for girls who didn't want to get out of bed in the morning? Where did I fit in?

I realized I wasn't just a kid—I was a girl, which was the

worst curse of all for a ball player. I thought about baseball every day. It wasn't the actual game I missed, but the feeling I had when I was playing.

The middle school years flew by, and I found myself a freshman in high school. I was uncomfortable in my own body. My brown hair was stringy and just sort of hung there, and I felt clumsy and uncoordinated. I even had to buy a bra, though my chest was as flat as my back. But I didn't want to be the only girl in the locker room not wearing a bra.

As a timid, self-conscious freshman, I didn't have many friends, so I spent my free time reading. Sometimes I read the novels the teachers assigned, but most of the time, I read sci-fi books about people with super powers. It was more interesting than reality. Reading books was a good way for me to hide from the world. I was so shy, I'd sometimes cut class and hide out in the library. Certain classes, such as Home Ec, required working in groups, and some days I wasn't in the mood to socialize. If it was Oral Report Day in English class, I'd be sure to skip. The high school librarian was old, and the stacks were over-stuffed with books, so by the time she figured out I was there in her library, the period was over. And teachers didn't seem to care when a quiet student cut class once in a while.

I hung out with a few guys because they were easier to be with than girls. Girls always made me feel inadequate, as if there was something wrong with me because I didn't care about shopping or which football player was hosting next weekend's party.

My only true friend was Justin Kennedy, a kid I'd known since I was five. His mother worked with my father. Justin was a junior in high school, so he was two years older than me. He was tall, even for a sixteen-year-old, and had longish brown hair. He hung out with the skateboarders, but he didn't have their slacker attitude. Justin was a really smart guy and accepted anyone as his friend. He always let me hang out with him and never made me feel uncomfortable. We'd known each other for years, so it was a given that we'd be friends. If it weren't for Justin, I probably wouldn't have made it through school. He was the only person who really understood me, and the only one who believed in me.

A couple days ago, Justin and his friends decided to go to the high school spring carnival. I didn't have anything better to do, so I tagged along.

Besides me and Justin, the usual three guys were with us: Ray, Adam, and Tommy. They were all juniors, same as Justin. Ray, a big tough guy, had a shaved head and a bad nicotine habit. Adam was basically Ray's wannabe and always carried a pack of cigarettes so Ray could bum them. Tommy had dyed black hair, and a skateboard in his hand at all times. He was a good skater, so we always dared him to do tricky stuff.

The carnival, which was in the dirt parking lot across from the high school, was full of the usual cheesy rides and games, including a Ferris wheel that looked as if it would break down at any moment. The jocks were decked out in heavy cologne and varsity jackets, trailed by giggling girls who wore belly shirts that said stuff like "hottie" or "trouble."

Stacy Downbaer, sporting a tight white shirt that showed off her huge boobs, claimed she was a "heartbreaker." She and I had hated each other since elementary school. It probably had something to do with the fact that she looked like a Cover Girl model, and I looked like a ten-year-old boy.

Justin and I were devouring a funnel cake when we spotted her at the "baseball throw" booth. Stacy was squealing to her boyfriend, Rick Bratton, "Win me the pink bunny, Ricky!" Stacy was a freshman, like me, but she thought she was Queen of the Universe because she was dating Rick, a junior and the most popular varsity baseball player in school.

"What kind of 'throw' game is this?" I said under my breath to Justin. "I think I'm going to *throw up*."

Giggling in his best "Stacy" voice, Justin said, "If you win it for me, I'll bounce up and down some more in my tight shirt."

"You two got a problem?" Rick asked, turning toward us.

Stacy glared at the two of us, her face all scrunched up. Then she put her arm around Rick. "Just ignore the skater scum and his lesbian hag," she said haughtily. "Win me the pink bunny."

Lesbian? Why had she said that? I felt my face growing hot with embarrassment. Was that what everyone thought—that just because I didn't spend hours fixing my hair and didn't wear trendy clothes that actually fit me, I must be a lesbian? I hated when people used that word, anyway. I wanted to lunge at Stacy and rub her face in the dirt. *That small-minded peon. Who did she think she was?*

I stepped toward Stacy, but Justin grabbed my arm.

"Let it go, Taylor," he said.

"I'm just going to rip out all her blonde hair, and then I'll be back," I muttered.

Still holding my arm, Justin said, "Wait, I have an idea." Just then, for the third straight time, Rick failed to win the pink bunny.

"Oh, boo," Stacy said.

"Want another three tries?" Mr. Sacamore asked from behind the booth's counter. I knew he was the hippie guidance counselor, but I'd never talked to him before.

That's when Justin spoke up. "I'll take three balls!" he said, walking up and paying his dollar. He took the three tattered baseballs and stepped toward me. Then, putting the baseballs in my hand, and jumping up and down, he squealed, Stacy-like: "The pink bunny, Taylor! Pleeeaaassee."

"I'm not doing this," I whispered to him, gritting my teeth.

"Why not?" He looked at me with sad eyes. "Because you know you can? Just do it, Taylor. Do it for me and the guys. I know you can. I remember seeing you throw balls in the yard when we were younger. You're good."

I hated the thought of anyone watching me and labeling me. If I won, what would they think? If I lost, what would they think? Struggling with those thoughts, I stood still for what seemed like hours. I gripped the ball tightly and ran my fingers over the stitches, like a blind person trying to read Braille. Strangely, the feel of the ball in my hand calmed me.

I approached the throwing line in front of the booth as if someone else were controlling my body.

"Whenever you're ready," Mr. Sacamore said.

I had three balls to knock down the three silver bottles. Each bottle was about a foot apart on the rickety shelf. There was no room for error. I placed two of the balls on the ground beside me. Holding the first in my right hand, I stared at bottle number one.

"Just throw it, girlie!" someone yelled from behind me.

I brought the ball back slowly, staring at my target, and then released it with all my might. *Smash!* The bottle fell, spinning to the ground. The crowd was silent.

"That's one!" Mr. Sacamore announced proudly. I leaned down and picked up the second ball. I brought my arm back, and then stopped. If I was going to do this, I was going to do it right. I leaned down and picked up the third ball as well.

With a ball in each hand, I simultaneously hurled them both at the two remaining bottles. The bottles not only fell, but immediately broke into pieces of glass.

"Holy crap!" Even Ray, tough guy that he was, covered his mouth in awe.

I walked toward Mr. Sacamore. "The big pink bunny, please," I said, pointing to it with a shaky hand.

He handed the bunny to me, his mouth gaping open. "We

have a big winner," he said as I walked away with my prize.

Justin practically hopped up and down like a bunny himself as I handed him the fluffy pink nightmare. "You're my hero," he said, grinning.

"Can we get out of here now?" I asked, pushing my way through the crowd.

"Whatever you say," Justin answered.

As we left the carnival, I was feeling . . . Actually, I didn't know how I was feeling. At first, I'd been angry and embarrassed, but now I felt like hugging Justin and kicking his bony butt at the same time.

"That was so awesome what you did back there," Ray said. "You made that jock look like an idiot. How'd you learn to throw like that, Taylor? You don't throw like a girl."

I didn't answer him. The truth was, I didn't know what to say. I guessed my dad or my brothers had taught me how to throw, but I had no recollection of being shown. When I'd played Little League, I'd figured it was something I was born being able to do.

"We have to hit up some more school carnivals," Ray said to Justin, patting him on the back. "Maybe we could even swindle some cash out of a few jocks next time."

All of a sudden, I felt the need to get away from everyone. I couldn't stop thinking about what had happened with Stacy at the carnival. She had been annoying me since second grade. I may have been an ugly, scrawny geek, but I didn't have to take crap from her. Her curvy body, long pretty blonde hair with highlights, and perfect cheekbones made me so angry. She was the girl all the guys drooled over, while I was just some girl who could throw. And now I'd have to go to school on Monday, and everyone would be talking about me. "Hey, did you hear about that weird girl—I'm not sure what her name is—who threw a baseball better than Rick?" I couldn't stand the thought of people saying those things about me.

As we crossed the next street, I started running. Ignoring the yells from the guys, I kept running until I was in my backyard. Out of breath, I slumped down on the ground. I sat there and cried for a long time, thinking about how strange I felt every minute of every day. I didn't belong anywhere. My family ignored me. School was a black pit of despair. My arms were too long for my body . . . I didn't know who I was.

Confused about my life and identity, I walked into the house and yelled "hello." No answer. Everyone was probably still at Danny's ball game. I opened the fridge, thinking I'd feel better if I ate, but nothing looked appetizing. I closed the door and leaned against the counter.

The kitchen was a mess—as usual. No one had taken out the trash or the recycling. Soda cans and beer cans were stacked next to the sink. I guess Dad was sending me message—that it was my turn to take out the garbage. But if he was going to come home and drink beer, he should have been the one to throw the cans away.

I pushed a few cans into the sink, feeling pissed. The cans had weird labels on them with words I couldn't pronounce. My

Uncle Ted visited us every few months and always brought my father beer from other countries he'd visited on business. "Here's a little something to help you get through the tough days," Uncle Ted always said.

I picked up one of the cans and stared at it. I wondered if it really did help people get through bad days. Justin always said drinking was for morons and made people stupid. But, at that moment, I didn't mind thinking less smartly. My problem—or at least part of it—was that I couldn't *stop* thinking.

I went back to the fridge and opened the door. A six-pack of beer was on the top shelf. I stared at it for a moment, then closed the door, but I didn't let go of the handle. My dad wouldn't miss it. I was fourteen—other kids my age drank. I opened the door again, grabbed the six-pack, and walked out the back door toward the lake behind the high school. I heard the school carnival winding down across the field. *Stupid carnival.*

Settling myself down against a big oak tree, I opened the second can—I'd finished the first one while walking there. I'd never drunk alcohol before, and I didn't know why I did it then. I suppose I just needed something to do besides throwing a baseball with all my might or trying to fit in with people who considered me an alien. By the fourth can, I found myself standing by the school's front door. I don't remember much more of that night, except for Justin walking me—more like carrying me—back home.

"Come on, Taylor, we have to get out of here," I remembered him saying, the faint sound of sirens wailing in the background.

The next day, which was a Sunday, I was awakened by the sound of my phone ringing—*loudly*. I covered my head with a pillow, hoping the annoying sound would stop. It kept ringing.

I bent over and picked up the phone from among my clothes piled on the floor. "Hello?" I said groggily.

"Taylor, it's Justin. Are you okay?"

"Yeah, I'm okay . . . except for the banging inside my head."

"What happened last night?" Justin asked. "Have you lost your mind?"

"I know, I'm sorry if I freaked you out . . . I know how you feel about drinking and stuff. Sorry you had to take care of me."

"Taking care of you is part of being your friend, idiot. What I'm concerned about is your butt getting thrown in jail."

"Why? Did someone see me drinking?" Justin's words had jolted me awake.

"I don't know if anyone saw you drinking," he said, "but someone probably saw you throwing bricks through the windows of the new science lab at school!"

I held my breath. "What are you talking about, Justin?" I got out of bed and went to look out my window, as if I was being watched.

"I guess you don't remember that part, huh, booze hag?"

I paced around the room and said, "You saw me do that? I, uh, don't remem . . ." Then it came to me. I stood still, remembering the pile of leftover bricks from the new gym . . . the shiny new glass windows in the science lab . . . the anger . . . feeling better watching the glass shatter . . . Was any of that true? I thought it had been a dream. I panicked. I had to go see for myself.

"Justin, I have to go."

"Wait, T," I heard just before I hung up. I quickly threw on my sweats and sneakers, and sprinted over to school.

When I arrived, two police officers were in front, talking to Mr. Sacamore, the guidance counselor, and Mrs. Sullivan, the principal. I ducked across the street and hid behind the trees.

"Out for an early run, Superwoman?"

I turned to see Rick, jogging up the sidewalk toward me.

"Yeah," I stammered. Oh, God. Of all the people I did not need to talk to right then, he was at the top of the list.

Rick slowed his pace, looked at me, then nodded toward the school. "Someone must have had a pretty good arm to reach those second floor windows," he said, sprinting away.

If the cops knew I'd thrown the bricks, why hadn't they come for me Saturday night? Did Rick really know it was me? I watched the policemen shake hands with the administrators and then get in their squad car. They did not turn on their sirens. I breathed a sigh of relief as they turned right out of the school driveway, heading in the opposite direction of my house. I was safe—for the moment at least.

The rest of that day, I hid in my room, nursing my headache, and periodically peeking out the window. I was waiting for the police to show up, waiting for my dad to bang on my bedroom door and scream at me.

But the cops never came, and, as usual, my dad never knocked.

CHAPTER 3

E arly Monday morning, when I entered the school building, I noticed that the broken windows were covered with silver duct tape and cardboard. I tried to ignore it—most kids ignored stuff like that. The adults were the ones who noticed, shook their heads, and said, "What's happening to today's youth?"

I assumed I'd gotten away with my vandalism because the police hadn't come to my house. And I was feeling safe, at least from the law, while I was failing my Algebra quiz during second period math class. Oh, what a sweet pleasure I got from screwing up another math quiz. I could've studied yesterday while lying low in my bedroom, but I didn't. I was so dumb.

In the middle of the quiz, the classroom door opened, and Mr. Horner, the Dean of Discipline, stepped inside.

"Sorry to interrupt, Miss Griffin," he said. "I need a moment with one of your students."

Oh, no. This was it. The hammer was about to drop. My luck had run out.

"No problem," Miss Griffin answered.

"Taylor Dresden," he said, scanning the room because he wasn't sure who I was. I looked up quickly, and he caught my eye. "Please come with me."

Oh crap, they knew. Mr. Horner marched me toward the office, past the secretary's desk, and into a small square room, which I assumed was the principal's office. The room had only one window and smelled like a musty basement. The walls and the floor were made of gray cement. Great. I was in the school's jail. "Wait here," Mr. Horner said, quickly closing the door behind him.

I sat down and put my head in my hands . . . *Dad was going to kill me.*

I ran my fingers through my stringy hair and tugged at the roots. Tears bubbled up in my eyes, but I blinked them back. *Look innocent. Maybe it's not about the windows.*

Like a trapped animal, I sat alone with my thoughts, with the anger I felt toward my father, and with the building disgust I felt about myself. This wasn't the real me. The real me wouldn't drink and destroy property. Who had I become?

Eventually, Mr. Sacamore, the peace-loving guidance counselor, entered the room. He was wearing his usual hippie outfit—blue jeans, a checkered flannel shirt, and those weird leather sandals of his. Everyone, including me, thought he was a weirdo. He always had a five o'clock shadow, and today, he smelled like the outdoors did right before it snowed, like clean air mixed with pine trees. I wondered what had happened to Mr. Horner.

"Taylor Dresden, I don't believe we've been properly introduced. I'm Mr. Sacamore," he said, extending his hand. I shook it, but I was confused by the nice-guy act.

"I have some good news and some bad news for you," he

said, sitting down and opening a manila folder. "Which do you want first—the good or the bad?"

"I guess . . . the bad," I answered.

"All right then, here it comes. I saw what you did Saturday night after the carnival," he said calmly, sitting back and folding his hands in front of him.

"Oh," was all I could manage.

He looked at me and waited.

"I guess I'm in trouble, huh?" I said.

"That depends, Taylor. You see, I'm the only one who saw you throw those bricks. And here comes the good news for you. I didn't report you to the authorities."

"You mean the police?"

"Exactly. I decided we could keep this between the two of us, but with a few conditions."

"Suspension?" I asked.

"Not exactly."

I squirmed in my seat. What was he planning to do to me? Whatever it was, I just hoped his plan didn't include telling my father.

"What, then?" I asked, not really wanting to hear his response.

"Well, there are two parts of my plan for you, Taylor. One involves you helping out the school. The other involves you helping out yourself."

"Okay," I said, confused.

"The first thing I need to know, though, is do you think you need help?"

"With what?" I asked.

"Anything," he said.

"I guess my grades need some help," I said, wondering what he was fishing for.

"That's it?"

I shrugged.

"What about how you feel about yourself? Do you feel good about yourself? Are you happy?"

No one had ever asked me that before. I was definitely not happy. I was downright miserable. But what did that have to do with me vandalizing the school? I sat in the old office chair and stared at my hands. Why should I tell this guy if I was happy or not? It wasn't as if he could change the way I felt.

"I guess I feel fine," I said, looking at the floor.

"Well, maybe I should start by explaining my plan. Let me begin by saying you have a choice. You can go along with my punishment, or you can decide not to, in which case I will turn you over to the police. Okay?"

"Yeah, okay," I answered.

"First, I would like to meet with you on a regular basis," Sacamore said. "I'd like to get to know you, talk with you . . . that sort of thing. How about coming to my office every Friday during study hall?"

"Uh . . . okay," I said. I guessed he wanted to do some sort of therapy with me. At least it was better than telling my dad or going to jail.

"And there's also a second part," said Sacamore. "I figure you owe something to this school, because you broke those expensive new windows, right?" He looked at me expectantly.

"Yeah, I guess so." I wondered where he was going with this.

"So, one of the things the school needs is help in the athletic department."

"You want me to clean the gym equipment or something?"

"No. What the athletic department could really use is a winning baseball season. They haven't had one in a long time."

"So, what does that have to do with me?" I said skeptically.

"They need a strong pitcher. I've decided that you'll pitch for them."

I snorted out a laugh. Was this guy a lunatic? He must've thought I was someone else. Then, I got defensive.

"That doesn't make sense, Mr. Sacamore. Number one, I don't play baseball. Number two, the team is for boys." I sounded like I was pleading with him to change his mind, but a part of me was strangely excited. I missed playing baseball. The sport was so easy for me, and everything else was so hard and complicated. But my fear of humiliation took hold of me, and I said, "Isn't there something else I could do to help the school?"

"Your other option is a ride in a squad car," he said firmly.

I spit out the words in a final plea, "But . . . I'm a girl."

"There's no rule against girls being on the baseball team. They've just never tried out before."

"I haven't played on a team since Little League, when I was

like eight years old," I protested.

"Listen, Taylor, relax. I saw you knock down those bottles at the carnival. You're a natural. Tryouts start Thursday after school. I'll let the coaches know you're coming."

Desperately, I asked, "What if I don't make the team?"

"If you try your best at tryouts, and they cut you, then we'll come up with a new plan."

I sat there, dumbfounded. The bell rang for third period.

"Hurry along now, so you won't miss any more class time," Mr. Sacamore said, ushering me to the door. "Remember, Thursday, after school, in the gym. I'll be watching."

I walked slowly back to class. I felt numb from what had just happened. I guessed I should be happy I wasn't going to the slammer for the rest of my high school years . . . but *baseball*?

For the past six years, I'd tried so hard to not think about baseball. When my dad or brothers watched games on TV, I avoided the family room. And I never went to any of Danny's Little League games. Heck, I even pretended I had cramps when it was baseball day in gym class. Now, this wacked-out guidance counselor wanted me to play. What a sick, twisted turn of events.

I entered third period five minutes late.

"Taylor, do you have a pass?" Ms. Clark asked as I walked slowly to my seat.

"No, I was in the office," I answered.

"If you cannot produce a pass, I will see you after school," she added in a matter-of-fact, case-closed voice. She turned back to the class. "Let's open up to page nineteen in our novel."

Great. An after-school detention—just what I needed with all my problems.

After lunch, I snuck out the back door of the school while everyone else was heading to the afternoon pep rally. I had to figure out what to do about this baseball thing. I couldn't play, could I? I mean, baseball was the only thing that ever made me happy, but playing now would be like letting my dad off the hook for what he'd said. By not playing, I figured, I'd be punishing him. I never told him I stopped playing to hurt him, though, and he probably wasn't hurt anyway. He was most likely thrilled that I quit. So the only person I'd be punishing was myself. I was in a daze by the time I pushed open my front door.

After school, Justin stopped by my house. He found me lying like a slug in front of an afternoon talk show.

"You actually watch this crap?" he asked.

"I'm not really watching," I said. "I'm trying to slip into a coma so I never have to go back to school again."

"What happened second period? I saw Horner taking you out of Algebra." Justin pushed my feet off the couch so he could sit down. "Did he know about the windows? Are you suspended?"

"Horner didn't know anything. But Mr. Sacamore saw the whole thing."

"That sucks," he said, shaking his head. "What are they

going to do to you?"

"Well, Sacamore said he wouldn't report me to the cops . . ."

"Oh, that's good."

"On two conditions."

"What?"

"That I meet with him every Friday . . . and that I try out for the baseball team," I said quietly and a bit embarrassed.

Justin laughed. "The baseball team?" he said. "Now, that's rich."

"I'm glad you think it's so funny."

Still chuckling, he said, "It's not funny, Taylor, it's just . . . well, most people would be happy they weren't suspended or arrested. You're moping around here when you should be celebrating about how easy you got off. Typical Taylor—seeing only the dark side of things."

"It's not easy, Justin," I yelled. I turned to him. "You don't understand about me and baseball. It's not easy for me to just pick up a baseball and start playing again." I was close to tears.

"So, you're out of practice. You can brush up after a little time playing."

"I don't want to play!" I screamed. "I hate the game, and I'm not doing it!"

"Why, T? What's the big deal?"

I was getting more and more upset. "You don't understand, okay?" I was practically screaming at my best friend.

He moved closer to me and put a light hand on my arm, trying to calm me down. Suddenly, I felt strangely weak and female, and pulled my arm away nervously.

"So, explain it to me, then," he said. "From what I remember, you're pretty good. You played when we were kids and—"

"Forget it," I said, heading toward the staircase. "I'm going to lie down. I feel sick to my stomach." I began to go up the stairs. "I'm not playing. I'll talk to you tomorrow."

"Taylor, I don't think you really have a choice," he said, sounding concerned. "Sacamore handed you a gift with this, so do it. I mean, really . . . consider the alternative."

I didn't answer him, but I did consider the alternative, which would make life with Dad even worse, if that was possible.

Justin watched me walk up the stairs before letting himself out.

CHAPTER 4

The next few days were total torture for me. All I could think about were the tryouts on Thursday. I couldn't sleep or eat. I couldn't decide if I should blow the tryouts or actually try to pitch my best. Would Sacamore know if I wasn't trying? He *did* see me throw at the carnival.

I didn't want to play, but I didn't want to embarrass myself in front of the coaches and students. Being on a team again wouldn't be too bad, though—it forced people to kind of be friends with you—but Rick would probably make sure no one talked to me.

By late Wednesday night, I still didn't have a plan or made a decision. I was wandering around the kitchen about ten o'clock, and my dad, as usual, was in his den reading. I munched on a piece of bread with peanut butter and stood outside the den, silently watching.

Dad always looked tired. In fact, I almost never saw him sleeping. He was up in the morning before me, and stayed up late into the night. I wasn't sure if he slept at all. He probably wasn't even human.

Dad was sitting at his desk with his reading glasses on the tip of his nose. He was forty-five years old, and he still had a full head of hair, but it was almost all gray, with only a few streaks of brown left. To me, he looked cold and mean—and he was. No matter what good things I did, nothing was good enough for him. Maybe this time he would be impressed with me. Baseball was the one thing he actually seemed to enjoy.

"Hi, Dad," I said, walking into the den.

"You still up?" he asked, keeping his eyes on the book.

"I can't sleep."

"Uh-huh," he mumbled.

A few moments passed, and I could tell he wasn't going to ask me why I couldn't sleep. I figured I had to tell him about the tryouts, in case I ended up playing on the team or dying from humiliation.

"I'm trying out for the baseball team tomorrow," I said quietly. "Pitcher."

Still engrossed in his reading, he said, "Don't be silly, Taylor. It's late. Go to bed."

"But Dad, I'm serious. I—"

"Taylor, it's late. I have a lot to finish here."

Throwing my hands up in frustration and slumping up the stairs, I went into my room and sat down in front of the mirror. I stared at my long, stringy brown hair. Dad never listened to me. He never said anything when I got good grades. He never said anything when I cleaned around the house. He never hugged me goodnight. He didn't care if I played baseball. I reached into my top desk drawer and pulled out the scissors. I began chopping off chunks of my hair—big chunks. He cared when my brothers played. More hair fell to the floor. Hot tears streaked down my face. He didn't love me. No one even cared that I was alive.

By this time, my hair was sticking out in every direction, like a punk weirdo's. Oh well, I had to wear a baseball cap anyway. I suddenly felt exhausted as I stared at my mowed hair in the mirror. But I felt better. For some reason, I fell asleep that night as soon as my head hit the pillow.

Thursday morning, I got up early and stuffed some gym stuff in my book bag. I didn't own a baseball glove, so I slipped into Brian's old room to find one. He was a freshman in college now, and Dad kept his room the way he'd left it. Brian came home only on the holidays, mostly to add to the laundry piles. Brian didn't play ball any more, which I thought made Dad mad. I peeked under the bed—nothing but dust bunnies.

I headed for the closet and opened the door, smelling the musty leather. I dug through the dingy sneakers and crumpled baseball cards. At the bottom of the mess, I unburied an old glove. It was as flat as a pancake and faded with age, but I picked it up and held it like it was a priceless vase. I slipped it onto my left hand and felt the soft bumps of the worn leather inside. *This will do*, I thought as I slammed my right hand into the glove's pocket.

I hurried down to the kitchen and grabbed a cereal bar from the cabinet. At the counter, my younger brother Danny was eating a large bowl of fruity cereal while Dad sipped coffee and looked out the kitchen window.

Danny stared at me, his mouth wide open. "Taylor, your hair

is crazy!"

Dad turned his head to look at me.

Laughing, I said, "Yeah, Danny, maybe I could borrow one of your baseball hats."

"I don't know if that's gonna help," he said, "but I'll get you one." He scooted off his chair and loped toward the hall closet. Danny was always able to smile through anything. He didn't know Dad hated me, and I never had the heart to tell him. Dad was his hero, and sometimes I thought I was the second person he worshipped. Now that Brian was out of the house, everything I did was the coolest. My biggest fan was a ten-year-old kid.

Dad took a long look at me. He reached into his pocket and handed me a few bills. "For lunch . . . and a little something extra for a new hat," he said, shaking his head as he walked into the den.

I smiled as I looked at the money. At least he noticed. "Forget the hat, Danny. I'll buy my own," I yelled, running out the back door.

I hurried toward town so I could buy a new hat before school started. Along the way, people gave me some odd looks. I must've looked insane. I shuffled into the Sports Depot store that had just opened. I stood in front of the wall of baseball hats, trying to decide which one to buy. I'd never been a fan of one team in particular, though my dad and brothers were hardcore Yankees fans. I moved along the wall. Tigers? Giants? There were also hats with silly pictures and phrases, like "Number One," and "Over the Hill." Then I saw it—the perfect one for me.

I reached up, pulled the pink hat from the wall, and took it to the register.

"Would you like a bag?" the cashier asked.

"Nope, I'm gonna wear it," I answered, pointing to my hair and making the man smile and nod.

I bent the brim, folded the hat in half a couple times, and plopped it on my head. Wearing my new hat, I walked toward school. On the way, I passed a couple of fourth graders. They pointed to my hat and read the logo aloud, "Girls Rule."

When I got to school, Justin was waiting for me at my locker. I took off the baseball cap and shook my head.

He looked at my hair and smiled. "Love the hat. And please, I must have the name of your stylist."

We both laughed.

"I guess you're ready for the tryouts then," he said.

"I'm nervous as spit, actually," I told him.

Trying to lighten the mood as we walked to first period, Justin said, "I didn't know spit got nervous."

I laughed. "Oh, it does. It certainly does."

"Well, I'll be there to cheer you on," he said, jumping around like a cheerleader. "We've got spirit, how 'bout you?" he yelled, pointing at me and getting kneed in the stomach by someone passing through the hallway. It always amazed me that Justin never got embarrassed. And it seemed as if he was immune to people bullying him, too. I wished I could be more like him.

I pulled him to his feet and dragged him away from the group of students who'd stopped to watch his performance. "Justin, knock it off," I whispered, my face hot with embarrassment.

"Relax. I'm just warming up for later."

I shook my head. "Justin, you're not really coming, are you?"

"Abso-frickin'-lutelty," he answered. "I wouldn't miss it."

"I'd rather you didn't, okay? I mean, it's not that big a deal. I'll be fine. It'll make me more nervous if you're there. Besides, I don't exactly know what I'm going to do yet."

"What do you mean *do*?" Justin asked.

"If I suck, then Sacamore can't force me to play, so maybe I'll just kind of blow it on purpose," I said, shrugging my shoulders.

Justin looked disappointed. "T, that's dumb," he said. "Why would you do that? Geez, for once in your life . . ." He stopped talking and quickened his pace to get ahead of me.

I hurried to keep him from passing me. "For once in my life *what*?" I asked.

The bell for first period rang. We were standing outside my Bio class, but I waited for his answer. He sighed and looked up, keeping his eyes away from me. "For once in your life, stand up for yourself, and do something to make yourself happy. Sometimes, I just don't get why you keep yourself in this dark hole, and, uh . . . I don't know, Taylor . . ." He stopped and tried to find the words. "I have to go," said Justin as he walked away with a sullen look on his face that I'd never seen before.

I sat down in class and wondered what that whole thing was about. I'd always thought Justin was against school sports and school spirit. What had gotten into him?

After eighth period, I hurried to the girls' locker room. No one was there because softball tryouts were on a different day, but I saw tons of boys pushing into the boys' locker room. Some of them were big and looked a lot older than me.

I walked into the locker room and found the locker I usually used for Phys Ed. I pulled on a pair of black sweats cut off below the knee, a soft, gray sleeveless t-shirt, sneakers, and, of course, my new hat. I stared at myself in the full-length mirror. I looked like an eight-year-old. The hat that had seemed like comic relief this morning now felt embarrassing. I turned it backward, then frontward again. Then I tossed it in an empty locker.

Maybe Mr. Sacamore wouldn't show up. He hadn't talked to me since Monday, so maybe he'd forgotten. But as I exited the locker room, my glove in hand, I saw Mr. Sacamore in the gym talking to the coaches. He remembered, all right.

When I entered the gym, I felt a lot of eyes watching me. The head varsity coach, Mr. Perez, was yelling, "All students trying out, sit on the bleachers. Come on, people. Let's move it!"

I sat a few rows up, a good distance away from the boys. I

felt safer being able to see everyone. I kept my head down, so if people were looking my way, I wouldn't see them.

It was obvious that Sacamore had talked to Mr. Perez about me. The coach started off by saying, "Okay, people, none of you are on the team yet. This is tryouts, and everyone's allowed to at least try out." He probably said that to keep anyone from asking, "Why is that girl here?"

Mr. Perez paced in front of us on the gym floor. "Some of you may make the junior varsity team, or, if we're really impressed, the varsity team. We're going to start with a warm-up run around the field, and then we'll have a short practice game. If I give you a red shirt, you're on the red team. No shirt, you're on the white team. I think we've all done this in gym class, so you know the drill."

He called out names and tossed out red shirts. "Banno, Shratter, Cominski . . ." I didn't get one. "Everyone else is the white team." Coach Perez then gave a little speech about trying our best and all that stuff. Finally, he said, "Let's head out!"

We sounded like a herd of elephants as all the boys, and me, hustled toward the gym doors. When we got to the fence, we all lined up against it. The coach pointed to the field. "Two laps around, and it's not a race. Just get yourselves warm!"

Warm? I was already sweating like a pig. As we ran our laps, I tried to keep up with the middle pack of boys. I wasn't going to sprint ahead like the three showoffs in front. One of the boys in the lead pack yelled back, "You all run like a bunch of girls!"

"Real original," I said, loud enough for a few boys running

near me to hear. One laughed, but the others just picked up the pace.

As they trotted ahead of me, I heard one of them say softly, "What is she doing here, anyway? Everyone knows girls can't play as well as we can. It's like a scientific fact."

He was probably right. Why did I agree to try out? Most likely, I was just going to humiliate myself.

After the laps, we were directed to the dugout area. There were probably forty boys trying out, so we couldn't all fit on the bench. I got stuck outside the dugout, and had to crouch down to see Coach Perez as he explained our next activity.

"This is my assistant coach, Coach Jefferson. He'll be in charge of the white team. I want everybody on the white team to head over to the visitors' dugout. He'll ask you what position you want to play, and you might or might not get it today. Not everyone can play first base. All positions are important, so take what you get."

"All right," Coach Jefferson said, "let's go."

All of us on the white team took seats in the visitors' dugout. I was still avoiding contact with everyone, and they seemed to be doing the same with me. The only kid who sat near me was Glen, an overweight kid who was the last one to finish the laps around the field.

"I'll come by and give you an armband with a number to wear," Mr. Jefferson told us. "Please tell me what position you're trying out for, and then find someone to warm up with."

I watched Mr. Jefferson coming down the line. He gave out

numbers and assigned outfield to everyone who didn't know what position they wanted. He was a tall, dark-skinned man with a Jamaican accent. Or at least I thought it was Jamaican. He was a lot younger than Coach Perez, and he gave me a huge smile when he got to me. It seemed like he was genuinely impressed I was sitting there, the only one wearing a bra in the whole group. "Okay, you're number ten. What position?"

"Pitcher," I stammered, reaching for my armband.

"Pitcher? . . . Okay. Uh, Fields!" he yelled at one of the guys heading out to the field. "You're up for catcher, so warm up with number ten here." He looked back at me. "Go warm up with Fields. You'll pitch the second inning—maybe more. We don't have many pitchers. Good luck."

Great. Dave Fields—Mr. Popularity, good-looking, smart, athletic. I sat behind him in Bio, where he never talked to me. I'm sure he was dying to play catch with me, the crazy-haired girl. As I walked toward him, his buddies snickered and turned their eyes away from me.

Fields was always the polite, kiss-ass type, and was probably trying to get on Jefferson's good side. Handing me the ball, he said, "I'll go down by the fence, and you can throw a few." He jogged off toward the fence, making a cross-eyed face to his friends as he went. I felt like a circus act.

All right, just get it to him. Don't try to throw fast, just straight. I paused a bit to focus on pitching.

"Okay, ten, I'm ready. Pitch one in!" Fields yelled.

I didn't wind-up—I just lightly tossed the ball to him. I felt so uncomfortable, I was tempted to run away and never come back to this school again. But the ball made it to the catcher. Fields, looking bored and unimpressed, tossed it back. This time I wound up, still not trying to throw hard. *Just get it in his glove*, I kept saying to myself. My second throw was a little outside, but it was close. Throwing hard was easy for me, but hitting targets was a little trickier.

Just when I was starting to feel comfortable, Coach Perez yelled, "Okay, let's get started. White team, you're up. Reds, take the field."

I jogged into the dugout and took a seat. Jefferson had said I'd pitch second inning. Great! I'd thrown two whole pitches. I was so *not* warm. I stuck my arm underneath a pile of towels. Maybe that would get the blood flowing.

Wait a minute, I thought. *I want to blow this tryout. Why am I taking things so seriously? All I have to do is look like I'm trying my best for Sacamore, and then I can get out of here . . . and go home . . . to my empty room . . . and to my dad, who ignores me.*

The first inning went by quickly. My red team scored a run on an error by the shortstop. When we were up again in the second, luckily, I didn't have to bat— Jefferson had said the coaches wanted to see as many players as possible, so pitchers wouldn't bat. I love American League rules!

But our team went three up and three down in our half of the inning. The red team had a pretty good pitcher. Now it was my turn. As I jogged toward the mound, my legs were shaking—I hoped no one could see that.

As I reached the mound, the first batter, Jon Dunn, was heading to the plate. Breathing heavily, I turned away from him, glancing toward the bleachers and wondering what to do. Should I throw my curve or hang a meatball? And then I saw my answer.

Despite what I'd said, Justin had come to watch. He was standing on the top row of the bleachers, wearing an Evansville High sweatshirt.

"Let's go, white team. Kick some butt!" he yelled and clapped, smiling right at me. I sucked back a smile. Even though I'd told him not to come, I felt better with him up there. At least people would know I wasn't a complete outcast. I did have one friend. Justin was the best guy in the world. He knew exactly how to make me feel better in any situation.

"Batter up!" someone yelled.

I turned to face Dunn and just sort of let the ball go. It was fast— really fast—but way over the catcher's head.

Oops.Dunn shook his head, looking impatient.

I took a deep breath. I thought about the old days of Little League— when I cared about nothing but having fun, when I was thrilled to get that jersey with my number eight on the back. I remembered after the games, waiting in the snack bar line with the whole team, still in uniform, so we could get our free snow cones. I really loved everything about baseball back then. As I wound up for the next pitch, I tried to be that girl—the girl with guts who was too young to know she had any.

I threw my second pitch. It slammed through the heart of the strike zone and made a loud thwap in the catcher's glove. Dunn swung and missed by a mile.

"I'd call that strike one," Coach Perez said quietly, smiling at Dunn. Strike one was quickly followed by two curveballs that hugged the outside corner, and Dunn went down looking.

"Aw, man," Dunn said, slamming his bat on home plate.

I looked over to the bleachers and watched Justin do his own private wave. Finally, a good moment. The next two batters never had a chance. The inning ended, and it was someone else's turn to pitch. I went into the dugout and collected my bag and jacket. I felt the need to flee. I walked over to the assistant coach and asked, "May I go now, Mr. Jefferson?"

"Yes, that's all we need to see, Taylor."

I began to walk away, but stopped, and took a few steps back toward Mr. Jefferson. "How'd I do?" I asked shyly.

"Well, to be honest, your pitches were in the right place. I'm just not sure about the rest of you. Heart is 90 percent of the game, if you ask me."

"So I guess you're saying 'no,' then."

"Practice starts Monday at 3:00 on Field Two." He smiled. "But make sure you bring your heart with you this time."

After he said that, my heart did a little dance inside my chest while my body stood still as a statue. I was on the team! I tried to keep my usually sullen game face, though, as I walked away.

Justin was riding up to me on his bike when I reached the parking lot. "Need a lift?" he said, pointing to the handlebars.

"Thanks," I said, smiling. "Thanks a lot." And I meant it.

We'd only gotten about ten feet when we came face-to-face with the side of Rick Bratton's car. Rick had purposely pulled in front of us as we attempted to leave the parking lot. Stacy was riding shotgun.

Now, as far as I knew, the only reason Rick hated me was because Stacy told him to. (And, yeah, okay, the carnival incident, too. That must've made Rick hate me even more.) And the only reason I thought Stacy hated me was because in elementary school, I was paired up with her as her reading helper, which basically meant she was an idiot who spelled "cat" with a "k," and I was supposed to tutor her. Of course, she ignored me the whole time, which was probably why the only thing she read, even as a high school student, was her horoscope. I thought this was a stupid reason to hold a grudge, but then again, you had to consider who held it.

"Hey, Kennedy," Rick said to Justin. "Nice ride."

Justin smiled and answered, "Why thanks, Rick. That's so very kind of you. Any time you need a lift, you know who to call."

I tried to contain my laughter. Justin never let anyone rattle him.

Rick inched his car forward. "Maybe you could drop your girlfriend off at the softball field next time," he said and sped out of the parking lot.

Justin shook his head. "He's a charming guy, isn't he?" he said.

"Sorry, Justin," I answered, swallowing the lump that had been in my throat since lunch.

"Eh, don't sweat it. In ten years, when he's married to the supermodel, and I'm working at my dad's carwash, he'll be sorry."

I cracked up. "I meant I'm sorry he called me your girl-friend."

He began pedaling down the sidewalk. "Did he? I hadn't noticed."

CHAPTER 5

When I got home, Danny and Dad were already devouring dinner—a pepperoni pizza and a bottle of soda—our usual supper-time fare. They stopped chewing long enough for a quick, "Where were you?"

I wasn't going to beat around the bush, so I boldly said, "Baseball tryouts." I grabbed a slice of pizza and plopped down on a stool.

Danny jumped up. "Really, Taylor? You tried out? How'd you do? That's so cool. Did you pitch?" I had to put up a hand to stop him.

"Coach Jefferson told me to be at practice on Monday, so I guess that means I made the team."

Dad's facial expression changed from one of non-interest to one of frustration. "Taylor, what's this all about? I thought you hated baseball. What brought on the sudden interest?"

I wasn't going to tell him the guidance counselor was blackmailing me, so I took the defensive route. "What the heck do you care? You never cared what I did before. Why the sudden interest?" I threw his words back at him—that would really annoy him.

"Danny, go upstairs," Dad said as he glared at me.

"Aw, man," Danny said and stumbled out of the kitchen.

"Young lady, I do not appreciate your choice of words *or* your tone. And I do not think this baseball thing is a good idea. Don't you remember how you got so tired of Little League that you quit before the season ended? Do you think it's fair to put another team through that? And this is high school. People take varsity teams very seriously."

If he wanted a fight, he got one. Now, I was pissed. I quit the team because I was bored? That's what he thought? The heck with him!

"You actually think I quit because I was bored? Are you that clueless?" I pushed my stool away from the counter. "I quit because I heard you say what an embarrassment it was having a daughter who could outplay any boy in the neighborhood. I was eight years old, and I thought you were proud of me, but you weren't. All you saw was a girl in a baseball uniform. You never said I was good. Well, I *am* good, and I'm playing, whether you like it or not."

He looked at me, his mouth open, with nothing to say.

"I've got homework," I said as I slung my book bag over my shoulder and headed upstairs. "Sorry I'm such an embarrassment," I mumbled, just loud enough for him to hear.

I tossed my book bag on the floor of my room. Homework—I couldn't even think about it. I flung myself on the bed and cried. Why did Dad hate me? No wonder my mother left. I wept until my sobs turned into a hacking cough. I had to stop crying because it felt like someone was piling bricks on my chest.

I sat up and grabbed the tissue that was crumpled up on

my desk from the last crying fit. I blew my nose and stood up to meet my messy face in the mirror. My eyes were puffy, like an old lady's.

I looked out my bedroom window. It had grown dark, and the moon was peeking through the clouds. I heard doors closing in the hallway—Danny's and then Dad's. I opened the window and sat on the sill to get some fresh air. Trying not to cry again, I breathed in the cool night air. My life couldn't go on this way forever. It just couldn't.

Somewhere outside, below my window, I heard a faint rustling that snapped me out of my emotional state. It sounded too big to be a squirrel. Then the noise came again, followed by a muffled "meow."

Leaving my misery behind, I hustled out of my room and out the back door in the kitchen, quietly, so I wouldn't wake or disturb anyone. I tiptoed around to the front of the house and stopped to listen again.

"Kitty, kitty," I whispered. It was funny how I was able to put all my feelings on hold because an animal was in need. The thought that there was something more pitiful than me must've gotten me motivated or something.

I crouched down, made a soft kissing noise, and peered into the dark bushes. Out of the shrubbery waddled a small orange puff ball, crying and shivering as it circled my feet.

"Aww. Hi there, little guy," I said, reaching down to pet the kitten. I picked him up, and he immediately clung to my neck for dear life. "What's wrong? You hungry, cutie?"

Hugging his little body against my chest, I snuck him into the kitchen. My dad would have my head if he knew I had a cat in the house. Ever since I'd begged to keep a stray cat, years ago, he'd claimed he was allergic. I'd never heard him sneeze, though, when we visited my aunt, who had a dozen cats. *Liar!*

The kitten cried loudly, and I shushed him. "Shh, you'll get me in trouble." I grabbed a bowl, filled it with water, and placed it on the counter, along with the kitten. I turned away from him and opened the fridge. What could I feed a cat? There was some leftover chicken wrapped in plastic wrap. I unwrapped it and started cutting it into little pieces on the counter. The kitten started licking and biting my fingers before I could finish cutting.

"Hey, okay. Here." I broke up the rest of the chicken with my fingers and tossed the pieces toward him. I watched him wolf down the small morsels and sniff the counter for more. Suddenly, I heard a door creak on the second floor. Uh oh. I scooped up the kitten and the bowl of water and maneuvered my way out the back door. Sitting down on the brick steps, I held the kitten up high and looked at his face. I wanted desperately to bring him upstairs to my room and snuggle with him for the night. Sometimes I felt so lonely in my own house. Nights were the worst. The hallway was full of closed doors—closed not to keep the person inside safe, but to keep everyone else out.

Again, I heard a noise from inside the house. Someone was coming downstairs. I put the kitten down and listened. The kitten scampered into the bushes, hopped up the fence, and scooted through the next yard.

"No," I said in a screaming whisper. "Come back." But he was long gone. He'd disappeared in the darkness, and I was alone again. Why did I get attached to lost kittens so quickly? He had been here for only a few minutes, but I was heart-broken. I sucked back my tears and finally retired to bed.

The next morning, I woke up groggy, still wearing my clothes and my sneakers. I peeked out my front window and scanned the yard for the kitten. No sign of him. Then I remembered I was scheduled to meet with Mr. Sacamore every Friday during study hall until I was cured or whatever. Great. I picked up my black hooded sweatshirt from the floor, threw it on over my t-shirt, and headed to school.

I sat in class all morning, zoning out and wondering what Sacamore was going to talk to me about. When study hall period rolled around, I took my sweet time getting to his office. After passing by his door three times, I finally stopped and knocked softly. *Here goes nothing*, I thought.

"Come in," I heard from the other side of the door.

I stepped in quietly and said, "Hi."

He just smiled and nodded.

"Taylor Dresden," I said, unsure why he wasn't speaking. "Remember?"

He gestured toward a comfy-looking chair and said, "Oh, I know who you are, Taylor. Have a seat."

I sat down on the end of the chair and placed my book bag between my legs. I looked around the room, waiting for him to talk, but he just sat there quietly.

The office was stuffed with books, pictures, and paintings. Some pictures were hanging up, and others were leaning against the walls. The overall effect was that of an organized mess. Everything had its own pile. His desk had a jar on it with different packets of weird herbal tea. The flavors had names like "Soothing Cinnamon" and "Raspberry Relaxation." Two brightly-colored stuffed bears were leaning against his computer. Long spider plants hung from the large window behind his desk, and the sun was leaving a glossy shine on the leaves. It was a warm, cozy room, especially compared to the gray hallway I'd just left. Maybe he lived in his office.

Sacamore was wearing jeans and a black sweater that was fuzzy from being over-worn. It seemed like hours before he said anything.

"So, how are you feeling today?" Sacamore said.

I nodded. "Fine."

"Did you do that yourself?" he said, pointing to my hair.

"Yeah," I answered shyly.

"Any particular reason?"

So my dad might notice I was alive. But I couldn't tell Sacamore that. "Nope."

"Okay." He waited a few long moments, then said, "Baseball practice begins next week?"

"Yep."

"How do you feel about it?"

What was he trying to get me to say? "A little nervous, I

guess."

Again he waited. Maybe he wanted me to say more, so I continued. "They put me on the varsity team."

"Are you happy about that?" he asked.

"Well, at least I don't know most of those guys, 'cause they're not in my classes."

I wasn't happy that Rick was on the team. I was sure Stacy would be coming to all the games. I wished Rick didn't know me.

"Not knowing anyone is a good thing?"

I shrugged. "It's easier when no one knows you. You can lay low, you know?"

Sacamore nodded a bit. "Tell me about your friends, Taylor," he said.

I shifted uncomfortably in my seat and looked at the floor. "What, like girl friends?"

"Girls, boys, whatever."

"Well, my only good friend is Justin. I don't really have any girl friends."

"That's okay, but why do you think that is?"

I shrugged. "I don't know. Girls don't seem to like me, I guess."

He waited for more. I didn't say any more. We sat there quietly for a while, and then he spoke. "Are you ready for your homework?"

What? He's giving me homework? "Homework?" I asked.

"Yes. We're in school, and you're a student, so I'm giving you an assignment."

"Okay," I said reluctantly.

"I want you to open up to someone. Anyone. Someone you already know or someone you just met. Over the next few weeks, show someone a little Taylor Dresden, and then see how you feel afterward. You don't even have to tell me about it."

Confused by his hippie-like weirdness, I asked, "Then how will you know if I did it?"

He smiled. "I'll know," he said.

Okay, whatever. Open up—sure, okay. We chatted for a few more minutes about baseball and my grades, and then the bell rang for lunch. We said goodbye, and I hurried down the hall to my locker, where Justin was waiting for me.

"How'd it go?" he asked.

"It was weird."

"You're weird," he said, teasing.

"You're a freak," I said back.

We headed toward the lunchroom. "You're freaky and weird," Justin said, "and your feet smell like Cheetos."

I started to laugh and punched him in the arm as we walked. Thank goodness someone could make me laugh.

I spent most of Saturday hiding in my room. On Saturday night, I had to get out of the house. I also felt like I should practice before Monday's team practice. I was far from being in shape. I grabbed Brian's glove and a flashlight, and snuck out the back door. Justin was at his dad's house for the weekend, so I couldn't visit him. I wasn't about to go anywhere near the school or its windows, so I headed to the park. I found a good-sized tree and figured it would make a perfect strike zone. Unfortunately, I only had one ball, so I had to throw the pitch and then run to pick it up. This was one reason why I needed more friends.

At least all the running would help me get in shape.

CHAPTER 6

Monday after school, I tried to get myself ready for baseball practice. Did Coach say to report to the weight room? Oh crap. I didn't remember.

I changed in the girls' locker room with the softball players. I felt the vomit building in my stomach. I was already so nervous about the team, and it was only practice. Trudy Harris, a sophomore, who was changing across the aisle, stared at me and then asked, "Are you on the softball team with us this year?"

"No, baseball actually," I answered, swallowing back the barf.

"Seriously?" She looked interested.

"Yeah, for the moment."

"Wow, great way to meet guys, huh?"

Oh, the thoughts that were running through my head. Should I call her an idiot or just let it slide? She was trying to be nice, and I was too nauseated to get into an argument with her. So I closed my locker, and walking past her, simply answered, "I guess."

She quickly added, "Hey, after games, we always meet for pizza across the street, if you wanna come some time."

"Oh, okay," I said, though I had no intention of going. I hadn't told Sacamore the whole truth when he'd asked me about girl friends. The truth was, girls made me feel uncomfortable. They were so feminine and talkative. Even when girls tried to befriend me, I kind of pushed them away. It was easier to be alone. The last time I had a girl friend was in elementary school—Latasha Hendricks. And the only reason I liked her was because she used to make the boys eat dirt. But then she moved. Too bad.

I went into the weight room. I was less nervous than I thought I'd be. I was there with a few skinny freshman pitchers and Mr. Jefferson.

"All right, Mondays and Wednesdays we're in the weight room," Mr. Jefferson said. "Tuesdays and Thursdays we scrimmage until the season starts. We have two weeks until our first game." He walked over to the free weights area. "I'm going to show you what exercises would be most helpful to you, and then you can experiment on your own. Just be careful you don't lift too much weight or you'll be too sore to pitch tomorrow." He ran through the exercises and posted a schedule on the wall. "Okay. Get to it."

I'd never lifted a weight before in my life. I stood there, like they'd just given me the Cy Young Award, as the boys jumped on the machines.

"Need some help, Dresden?" Mr. Jefferson said to me.

No one had ever called me by my last name before. I liked it. "If you don't mind," I said.

He laughed and said, "That's why they pay me the big bucks." He showed me what to do, one step at a time. He made small talk with me as he taught. "You're right-handed, right? You have a mean curve, I hear." I wondered why he was being so nice. Maybe the evil guidance counselor, Mr. Sacamore, had threatened him.

After a while, I was actually starting to get comfortable with the weights. Lifting them made me feel strong. I liked the idea of being tough—usually I felt like a weak mess.

After the workout, I saw a few of the boys talking to each other by the pull-up bar. One of the taller ones was shoving another guy in my direction. Oh great! Now what? The kid headed toward me. I pretended to tie my sneakers and not notice him. He sat down on the bench next to me.

"Hey," he said.

I answered suspiciously, "Hi."

"So, what are you doing here . . . exactly?"

"What do you mean?" I asked.

He shrugged. "Well, why aren't you on the softball team?"

Because Sacamore's framing me—can't say that, though. I quickly came up with some feminist bull. "Because I don't play softball, I play baseball. Is there any law against girls playing baseball, or is this America?"

He looked shocked. He was speechless. I was shocked myself that I'd actually said that.

I stood up, grabbed my towel, and headed back to the locker room, trying to hold back the tears. When I reached the locker room, I went into the last bathroom stall, sat down on the floor, and cried. How was I going to play on this team? None of these guys wanted me here.

I stayed in the stall until I heard the softball girls filtering back in to take showers. I stood up and brushed myself off, wiping my face with my sweaty shirt. *Toughen up, Dresden.* I punched the stall door as hard as I could—with my left hand, of course. *Stop acting like a girl.* I held my head up and walked bravely out of the bathroom.

On Friday, I had another meeting with Sacamore. He was on the phone when I walked in, so I just wandered around the room looking at his weird collection of crap. The shelves were full of pictures. Some were in frames, and some were just laying there, their edges beginning to curl. I was still feeling bummed out about the weight room incident on Monday, but I didn't want Sacamore to know too much. I felt like less of a loser if I made it hard for him to drag information out of me.

I picked up a photograph of a bunch of kids and an older man sitting in a boat docked on the beach. I figured it must be Sacamore and his family when he was a kid. The side of the boat said "OCBP."

"Okay, thanks for calling. Talk to you soon," Sacamore said and hung up the receiver.

"Is this Ocean City?" I asked, walking toward him with the picture.

He took a peek. "I don't know. Could be, I guess."

"You were too young to remember?"

He stood up and moved toward the wall of photographs. "No, I'm not in that picture."

"Oh, who are they?"

"You got me. I just like the picture."

I placed the picture back on the shelf. "Okay," I said, waiting for him to say something more while I shook my head. This guy got weirder and weirder. "So why do you have it?" I said after a long stretch of silence.

He straightened a few of the pictures that were about to slide off the shelves. He smiled at one of them. "This one's cute," he said, showing me a picture of a black puppy.

"Uh-huh," I said. "So why do you have these pictures?"

"Students like to look at them, and I can tell a lot about the kids by the ones they ask me about."

I was still holding the boat picture. "Oh yeah, like what?" I asked, putting the picture back down.

He immediately picked it up. "Well, what was interesting to you about this picture?"

This guy was sneaky. But I played along. "I guess they look like they're all having fun," I said, walking over to take another look at it. "A group of kids and the dad enjoying the day."

"How do you know the man is the dad?"

"Just assumed. You know, kids on the beach . . . usually a parent would be there."

"Do you have any pictures like this?" he asked.

I sighed, sitting down in the brown corduroy chair. "Not that I know of."

"Why do you think that is?"

"Umm, 'cause we never go anywhere together as a family, and I don't have ten friends," I said, feeling pissed. "Is that what you wanna hear?"

He paused for a while and looked at me. "Taylor, I'm not your enemy. We're just talking . . . Did something happen this week to upset you?"

"Just boys giving me some sh—" I cleaned up my words quickly, remembering I was in school. "Just guys on the team, asking what I was doing there and why I wasn't playing softball. You know—typical macho guy stuff." He nodded. "Just remember, they're as confused and afraid of you as you are of them."

"Yeah, I bet," I said sarcastically.

"It's true. It's easier to say you don't like the new person than to take the time to get to know what they're all about. That's why in movies, aliens are always bad guys. Unfortunately, humans tend to fear differences instead of embracing them. You're different, Taylor, but eventually, that's what you'll find comfort in."

Huh? My brain was swelling—Sacamore and his philosophies. Maybe someday I'd know what the heck he was talking about. But, for now, the bell was ringing and I said my goodbyes. As I closed the door behind me, I had to swallow the lump in my throat. It seemed as if I'd had the same lump stuck in there since I first met Sacamore.

The next week flew by. I practiced with the team every day after school and met with Sacamore again on Friday to "talk." I wasn't sure if the talking was helping, but all the practicing made me too tired to think about how crappy my life was, so that was good. I stuck mostly with one catcher during practice—Louis. He didn't really have a choice about catching for me, and he was low on the popularity scale, so he wasn't a complete jerk to me. The coaches kept watching me closely, and I often saw Sacamore monitoring me from the dugout, casually questioning the coaches.

On the last practice day before our first game, I was in the locker room, packing up my gear, when Trudy Harris started talking to me again as if we were best buddies. It was probably because I was the only one left in the aisle, and she needed a warm body. Trudy was a little on the chubby side, and she was at least a foot shorter than I was. She was reaching up to her locker while trying to put her shoe on with the other hand. It was kind of a circus act.

"Hey, Taylor, right?" she asked.

I looked up from the bench and said sarcastically, "Yeah. Trudy, right?"

"Uh-huh. Good memory," she said. "So is that guy Justin your boyfriend?"

This was amusing. "Justin?"

"Yeah, the guy with the longish hair, who's really sweet?"

She thought Justin was sweet. Wait until I told him that. "You think Justin is sweet?"

"Oh, sure. I mean, he's one of those guys who looks kind of scary, with the dark grungy clothes and all, but in chemistry class, he always helps people out. One time, when we were lab partners, he cleaned my whole station." She moved closer to me and sat down. "I always see you with him, so I figured you were a couple."

A couple? I'd never thought about Justin that way. He was just a great friend. Was she asking me to hook her up with him? I hated when Justin had a girlfriend. The last girl he went out with was a real pain in the ass, and I hardly ever got to see him when they were dating. I couldn't let that happen again. "Are you interested in him?" I said.

Shaking her head, she answered, "Oh, no way. He's not my type. I've got my eye on this guy who's on the student council, actually. I was just curious about the two of you."

I responded quickly, "Well, we're just really good friends. We've known each other all our lives."

She fiddled with her lock. "Too bad," she said as she got up to close her locker. "I think you guys would make a cute couple."

Did she just use the words "cute couple" and me in the same sentence? This girl was a loon.

"Well, I have to get going," she said, throwing her bag over her shoulder. "I've got to feed my new kitty. He's so adorable," she squealed. "Do you like cats?"

I thought about the kitten I'd found in the yard a couple weeks ago. "Sure. In fact, I found a stray a few weeks ago, but I haven't seen him since. My dad wouldn't let me keep one anyway."

"It wasn't an orange tabby, was it?"

"Yeah, actually," I said surprised.

"One white foot?"

"I think so."

She laughed and nodded her head. "That was definitely my Trixie. He runs away like every other night. I think your house is only a few blocks from me."

I nodded, though I had no idea where she lived. I was happy that the kitten was okay, but kind of pissed that it belonged to Trudy.

"You should come over and see him sometime," she suggested.

Leaning down to tie my shoes, I gave my usual response. "Maybe."

"Remember, next week after games, we do pizza at Lou's Place."

I just nodded. *Sure.*

After she left, I thought about what she'd said. Justin and I a couple? Funny. I considered telling Justin about the conversation, but I figured nothing good could come of it. Either he'd laugh and say, "Yeah, right? Me and you, a couple?" Or he'd say . . . What *would* he say? Was the idea that crazy?

CHAPTER 7

Evansville High School's varsity baseball team was famous for only one thing—losing. They hadn't had a winning record for the past ten years. It was one of those losing streaks that seemed to last forever. Today—the first game of the season—we were playing Highland Regional. Though it was still April, it was a hot, humid day.

I was hanging out in the locker room before the game, dressed in my uniform, staring at myself in the mirror. Uniforms didn't lie. Now it was real. There was no doubt about it. I was on the baseball team. And I was afraid to go out to the field.

"Looking good, Taylor," Trudy Harris said as she pulled her hair into a ponytail. "Your uniform is so much better than ours. You have real jerseys. All we get are these cheap t-shirts. I'm so jealous." She pulled on her t-shirt. "Why'd you pick number 8?"

I slapped my hand against my glove and answered, "Eh, no reason. Just a number, I guess." But I did have a reason. I had been eight years old the last time I'd played baseball on a real team. And I was eight the last time I'd felt sure about myself. I'd give anything to be eight again. Of course, I couldn't throw like this when I was eight. But I could now. I started to feel a small thrill run through me. Though I wasn't scheduled to pitch today, I felt it—the feeling that made you all of a sudden run as fast as you could . . . the feeling you got when your favorite team scored that winning run . . . Okay, now I was ready to venture out of the locker room.

Trudy and the softball team were also heading out. "Wait up," I yelled to Trudy. I figured I could walk out with them and not look so lonely.

I jogged to the dugout on our field.

"Okay, everybody get in here and sit down," Coach was yelling. "Time for the first game talk."

I was trying to squeeze onto the bench, but no one was making room for me. The coach, standing with his hands on his hips, was eyeing me impatiently. Every time I'd try to sit, someone would move to block the space. It was like a bad game of musical chairs, and I was the only one still standing.

"Dresden, find a seat," Coach said quickly.

My efforts to get onto the bench were still being blocked by the boys.

"Whatever it takes, Dresden. Get a seat," said a very frustrated Coach. "Do it!" He was raising his voice now.

I was so embarrassed. I had to get a seat before my face turned purple. I spotted Joey Zeigler. He was a really short kid who lived next door to Justin. He reminded me of my little brother. I aimed right for him.

"Excuse me," I said and shoved his leg over with my glove, forcing him sideways. All the boys cracked up.

"Hey, Zeigler, she played you!" someone yelled.

The coach was pissed. "I don't know what you guys are

laughing at! You think that's funny? No one here has proven themselves to me yet. I don't care if you're male or female, or blue or green. This is a team, and if we're going to turn this team around, then you'd better start acting like one. If anyone has a problem with that, please speak up now."

No one said a word. I thought I'd stopped breathing. I knew they didn't like me. They looked at their feet and gloves. No one looked at me. I'd never felt so uncomfortable being the only girl on the team. For a moment, I wished I was on the softball team. But just for a moment. And then the game began.

Watching from the dugout was a thrill. I could hear everything the players said on the field. The "tink" sound the aluminum bat made when a player hit the ball was ringing in my ears. Just the thought I was going to pitch the next game was keeping me interested. The team's performance, however, was disappointing.

By the middle of the second inning, we were already down by two runs. Carlos Fiero was pitching for us and came into the dugout cursing and kicking at things. I remained quiet and sat at the very end of the bench. Rick Bratton was up at the plate, and he actually got a hit—our first of the game.

"All right, Rick," the guys yelled as he rounded first.

I didn't feel like I was allowed to cheer for any of my teammates. But I wanted us to win. Unfortunately, we lost 6-3. I walked back to the locker room in my clean uniform. I knew that if we were going to win the next game, I'd have to be really good. Obviously, this team wasn't good at scoring runs, and

because of the lack of quality pitchers, I was in the regular rotation. When I pitched, I'd just have to keep the other team from
scoring any runs.

CHAPTER 8

The Friday after our first home game was another Sacamore day. When I got to his office, he was sipping his herbal tea and fooling around with the CD player on his computer. The herbal tea smelled like honey and apples, and it made my stomach growl. I eyed the dish of chocolates on his desk.

Sacamore took another sip of tea. "Thirsty, Taylor? I could make you a cup if you'd like."

I still wasn't sure about this guy. "No thanks," I said. "But can I have a piece of candy?"

"Of course," he said, pushing the dish toward me.

I gulped down a piece and wished I could take another. But I didn't want Sacamore to think we were buddies or anything.

As usual, he was chipper. "So, I hear you're pitching the next game."

"Yeah."

He finally stopped fiddling with the computer and turned toward me. "Are you nervous?"

I was so nervous I hadn't slept in days. "A little," I said.

"Hmm. Well, how about I tell you a story? It might make you feel better."

"Sounds good to me. I always feel like I'm the one who has to talk in here."

He laughed and pushed the dish of chocolates toward me. "You just sit and relax."

I took another piece of candy and settled myself comfortably in the overstuffed couch.

"I grew up in Michigan—East River, a little town by the lakes. The only good thing about the town was that it was so cold, the lakes were always frozen over."

"That's a good thing?" I chimed in.

"I thought you were just listening," he said, pretending to be annoyed.

"Sorry." I rolled my hand for him to continue and then unwrapped more candy.

"Anyhow, it was good for me because I loved to play ice hockey. My older brother was always on the lake with his friends, and I was always begging him to let me play with them. But he said I had to be at least ten before the guys would let me participate."

I put my feet up on the coffee table, trying to see how much Sacamore would let me relax. "Thrilling story so far, Mr. Sacamore," I said sarcastically.

He got up from his desk and sat next to me on the couch. "I'm getting to the point. Take a chill pill."

He was so corny. But I was entertained and comfortable.

"So, finally, the day came. I turned ten February 18th—in the dead of winter. As usual, the lake was frozen. I suited up, taped up my stick, and followed my brother out the door that morning. He warned me about certain guys I should stay away from, and told me to keep my head up. That was his phrase—'Keep your head up, Luke.' I can still hear him saying it."

His first name was Luke. Weird. "So, what happened?" I asked.

"Oh, so now you're interested?"

I smiled and tested him with, "Come on, Luke."

He pointed his finger at me. "Watch it, sister."

"Sorry. Go ahead, Mr. Sacamore," I said and bowed in his direction.

"That's enough candy for you," he said, sliding the dish away from me. "So, I got down to the lake. The guys let me play on my brother's team. As soon as they dropped the puck, I skated like a madman toward it. I was cruising so fast, I forgot what my brother had said, and I didn't see Wayne Bracco coming at me from the right. Blam!" He stood up and pretended he was checking me into the boards. "I fell flat on my face. My front tooth went sliding across the ice, leaving a thin trail of blood."

"Ooh, that must've hurt," I said, wincing.

"You bet your butt it hurt."

"So, then what happened?" I asked. "You played anyway and scored the winning goal?"

"Nope. I started crying, and my brother had to take me home," he said, leaning back on the couch.

I was confused. I'd thought this story would have some great moral that was going to help me with my game. I shook my head and asked, "That's it? That's the whole story?"

"Pretty much."

"I don't get how this story is supposed to help me with my game."

"Well," he said slowly, "I learned something that day."

"What?" I asked, waiting for the big lesson.

"Even though I lost my tooth and only played for ten seconds, it didn't change the fact that I loved hockey. Messing up out there couldn't take away the thrill of finally getting the chance to play. It couldn't take away the feelings I had all those years of wanting to get out on the ice. And that's what sports are all about—the desire to try, not whether you win or lose."

I smiled. "Oh, it's that old 'not whether you win or lose' saying."

Sacamore leaned forward. "But you have to remember," he said, "that *how* you played the game isn't as important as the fact that you actually played it."

I laughed. "So you're saying it's okay if I suck?"

"Exactly," he said, relaxing back onto the couch.

I nodded at him, half confused about what Sacamore had just told me, and half relieved that the bell was about to ring. He sat on the couch, smiling at me. I liked the way his eyes crinkled when he smiled.

"So, you're telling me I'm going to bomb when I pitch?"

He shook his head. "I'm telling you it doesn't matter if you do."

The speaker above my head shook as the bell sounded for next period. I jumped a little when I heard it. I grabbed my book bag and walked slowly toward the wooden door.

"Bye, Mr. Sacamore," I said, opening the door.

"Bye, Taylor. Have fun out there."

CHAPTER 9

We'd lost our first game at home last week, and now we were at our first away game. It was my first game as a high school pitcher—a *girl* high school pitcher. I thought if I tucked my hair under my hat, maybe no one would know I was a girl. "Taylor" could be a boy's name, I figured.

The guys on my team still didn't talk to me. None of them had been outright mean, though—at least not yet. Curtis, the shortstop, told me they all figured they should keep their mouths shut because Coach Perez had threatened to kick their asses off the team if they didn't act like "team players." Hey, it worked for me. I preferred to be unseen and ignored.

I jogged out to the mound, and it became obvious that everyone knew I was a girl. The stands were crowded and noisy. So many people were squeezing onto the bleachers, I could barely see any of the silver metal showing through. As the first batter entered the box, someone from the crowd yelled, "Take the bitch deep!" In response to the profanity, a teacher ran over to the disruptive student and asked him to leave, which he didn't.

I wasn't offended by it, but it made me realize how ridiculous this whole thing was. I was going to pitch my game and then get out of there. Sacamore was right. Baseball was supposed to be fun, the way it was when I was little. We got older and turned everything into these *big deals*. Why was it that the more we learned and experienced, the dumber we got?

I looked up to the bleachers and saw a few kids from my school on the visitors' side, including Justin and my brother Danny. How'd *they* get here?

Then I realized everyone was waiting for me to pitch. I wondered how long I'd been daydreaming. I gathered up my strength and began the game by hurling the ball toward the plate.

"Strike one!" the umpire yelled.

The batter stepped out of the box and shook his head. I'd never thrown so hard in my life. I quickly wound up and delivered another pitch, a curveball.

"Strike two!" the umpire bellowed.

I lifted my hat slightly and pushed my hair back under it. I turned and threw a fastball toward the batter. He swung and popped out.

Yes! One out!

The rest of the first inning was easy enough—a fly ball and a groundout. And the next two innings went fairly easily, too. In the fourth inning, though, I walked the first two batters and was facing the clean-up hitter. I had been throwing good stuff. My pitches had been catching the outside corner of the strike zone, and many of the batters weren't swinging at them, hoping for a walk. This inning, it seemed as if the umpire had turned on me. The pitches he'd called strikes before were now balls. *Hometown sexist umpire!* How was I going to get out of this? I should've let Sacamore call the cops on me.

The umpire called four balls in a row as the number four batter stood there, barely lifting the bat off his shoulder. "Shoot," I
mumbled to myself as I paced around the mound. "Those last
two were perfect strikes." A few boos went up from our dugout
as the batter trotted to first to load the bases with only one out.
Coach Perez emerged from the dugout. I thought he was coming to take me out, but instead he approached the home plate
umpire.

"What was wrong with those last two?" he asked the ump.

"I call them like I see 'em, Perez. Always have."

"Well, maybe you need to start looking closer, 'cause the girl
is throwing dead-on strikes."

"Talk to your pitcher or get back in the dugout," the umpire
said.

Perez threw his hands up and headed toward me. He put his
arm on my shoulder and turned me toward the outfield. "Listen,
this guy's not going to call strikes on your curveballs, so just
throw fastballs and hope the batter makes contact and grounds
out."

"But my fastball's not going to have anything on it. He'll
crush it," I said.

"Just force him to keep the ball on the ground. I smell double
play," he said, then jogged back to the dugout. He smelled right.
The next batter grounded into a double play to get us out of the
inning. Yes! I slammed my hand into my glove as I hustled off
the field. How'd you like that, stupid ump?

During the next few innings, the umpire still called a lot of balls on me. By the end of the seventh inning, the score was 1-1. Perez took me out and put in Frank Lowell to close the game. I was annoyed because I hadn't won or lost the game. I'd proven nothing to the team or to myself. I sat by the wall in the damp dugout and watched Frank give up two runs in the bottom of the ninth. We lost—again. I felt all alone as I boarded the bus to go back to school.

Not one person said a word to me. I sat in the front of the bus next to the cooler of Gatorade and the equipment. Coach Perez was busy with his stats book, so I just sat and stared out the window. It was pretty sad when you looked for someone who'd talk to you, and you knew the only person who would was the teacher. And he got paid.

The bus was really noisy. The guys were complimenting each other on their few hits and Rick's stolen base. I was listening to them, but trying to act like I wasn't, and then I felt it—something had landed in my hair. I wanted to reach back to see what it was, but I was afraid. They wanted me to grab for it. I pretended I hadn't noticed and just sat there frozen. I wanted to cry, but I sucked it up. Twenty minutes went by. I never moved.

When we reached the school parking lot, I flew off the bus as soon as the doors opened. If everyone was going to laugh at me, I didn't want to hear it. I ducked around the side of the building and used my fingers to feel my hair. *Gum!* I yanked at it and cursed as I tore at a clump of hair. But it was stuck. Oh great, as if my hair could look any worse. Why did they hate me? I'd done my best. Why'd I have to get drunk and throw those stupid bricks? Hadn't I suffered enough?

I snuck through the back door of the school and into the locker room. I stopped to listen for any movement. Good, no one was here. I had to get this gum out before it left a permanent knot in my hair. But it wasn't the knot in my hair as much as the knot inside my chest that was causing tears to form in my eyes.

Wiping my eyes with the back of my hand, I stood over the sink to examine the damage. I remembered Justin's mom doing something with an ice cube years ago to get gum out of his brother's hair. Cold water maybe? I turned on the faucet and splashed cold water at the ends of my hair, but the gum was too far back for me to see what I was doing. As I battled with my mess, I heard a creak at the other end of the locker room. The door! Shoot, was someone in here?

"I think I left it in my locker. Just give me a sec to check," the voice said. Someone was walking toward my end of the locker room, and the second person seemed to be holding the door open, from the look of the shadow running across the floor behind me.

I stood frozen. She was getting closer.

The footsteps stopped. "Taylor? Is that you?" I recognized Trudy's voice.

I turned around to glance at her and tried to act normal. "Oh, hey, Trudy."

She moved closer. "You okay?"

"Yeah, I just got gum stuck in my hair. I guess it was on the back of the bus seat or something. I dunno . . ." I stammered.

She walked up behind me while I stared at myself in the mirror. It was so obvious I'd been bawling before she came in, but she pretended not to notice. "Ooh, that sucks. I have just the thing for that, though."

"Trudy," the girl at the door yelled. "You coming?"

Trudy turned toward the door and yelled, "You go ahead. I have to pee and stuff. I'll meet you over there."

The springs of the locker room door squeaked shut.

"Don't move," Trudy said. "Let me get my purse." She hurried her short body out of the bathroom area and returned quickly with a huge bag. After rifling through the bottomless pit for a while, she pulled out a tube of gel. "This should do it," she said, waving the tube. I was silent. I was afraid if I talked, I'd cry.

Trudy proceeded to squeeze out a huge glob of clear gel into her hand. It smelled like peaches and vanilla. Then she slathered it on the gum and smushed it all around. "Okay, hold still." She took a big brush and ran it through my hair toward the gum. I felt it stop, and I winced as it pulled at my scalp. "Sorry," she said sympathetically. "No pain, no gain, right?"

I forced a smile. "Go ahead," I said softly.

There was a loud rip as she pulled the brush through my hair. She held up the brush, which held quite a bit of my hair, and more importantly, the nasty piece of chewed gum. "Got it!" she said.

I felt the back of my head. It was sore but gum-free. "Thanks," I said, still fighting my need to cry.

"See, I'm good for something," she said, pointing at the brush full of gum and tangled hair.

"I'll get you a new brush," I offered.

"Oh, no need. I have tons." She opened her bag to show me a massive quantity of hair products, brushes, and clips.

I stood there awkwardly, not knowing what to do. I was glad the gum was gone, but I felt uncomfortable, thinking I had to stay and talk with Trudy when I really needed to run away and hide. I couldn't think of anything to say. As if she could read me, she said, "Well, I have to run. I'm late."

"Oh, okay," I said. "Thanks again."

As she walked toward the door with her huge purse, she stopped and turned. "Hey, Taylor?"

I glanced over at her.

"I just want to say that there are a lot of jerks in the world, especially guys, but not everyone is like that."

I felt the tears come back, and I looked down at the floor. Trudy seemed to understand what I was going through, and she kindly left the locker room so I could cry.

After what seemed like hours of isolation, I wrapped my coat around me and walked toward Justin's house. I didn't want to face my dad when I was in my uniform and upset like this. He'd only make me feel worse.

CHAPTER 10

Justin's mom was a great cook. She always made delicious food that was good for watching movies and lounging around. When I turned into Justin's driveway, I could smell nachos and chicken wings. I tapped on the screen door to the kitchen, thinking I must've looked like a mess.

"Hi, Taylor. Come on in, honey," she said as she wiped the counter. "Justin's down in the basement, as usual."

"Thanks, Mrs. K," I said.

"How was the game?" she asked.

I just shrugged and said, "Okay." I didn't feel like getting into details.

"You look like you could use a shower and some of my super nachos."

"Yeah, would you mind? I have my clothes and a towel and everything with me. I didn't get a chance to shower at school."

She shook her head. "Feel free. Go on up and get clean. I'll tell Justin you're here."

Being nice obviously ran in this family. I hurried up to the bathroom and thought how glad I was I'd come over here. I felt better already.

After I showered and ate, I headed down to the basement and joined Justin. He was watching *The Matrix* for the four zillionth time.

I didn't feel like telling him about the gum incident. I figured it would make me feel worse to rehash the whole thing. So I just sat back and tried to enjoy myself. Justin's basement was probably my favorite place to be.

After an hour or so, I started to become very aware of him leaning against the same pillow I was leaning against. My arm was killing me from the game earlier, and it was propped up on the pillow so my hand was inches from his cheek. When I moved my hand, I let it brush his cheek. I don't know why I did it.

He looked up at me and smiled. "Does your arm hurt?"

"Nah."

"Oh, that's right. You're a tough girl."

"It hurts a little, but it's fine," I said, finally giving in to the pain. "Got any ice?"

Hopping up from the couch, he said, "I'll bring you some of my best ice, madam!" He hurried up the basement stairs and quickly returned with two large bags of frozen peas. "Will this do?"

"Perfect. I love peas." I secured the bags around my elbow as Justin sat back down on the couch.

"What else do you love?" he said, way too seriously.

"What do you mean?"

Justin shrugged. "I'm just breaking your chops. Watch the movie, girlie."

I continued to stare at the side of his face. I examined the dark shadow on his upper lip and chin. He needed a shave. I watched him tuck his longer strands of hair behind his ear and smile at the screen. Wait, what was I doing? Why did he say that? Was he hitting on me? Justin? my friend?

I reached toward his face with my good arm and touched his cheek again. This time, I let my hand linger there. Without looking at me, he laid his hand lightly on top of mine. I felt really warm and really weird. Our two hands then played a little game back and forth for a long time. I'd never felt this way before. How could touching someone's hand feel so good? What was going on? Were we hooking up?

The peas were starting to thaw and drip all over the pillow. I took the bags off and tossed them onto the side table. Justin slowly reached for the pillow that was between us. I swallowed the thrilled lump in my throat. He was going to kiss me. What if I was bad at it? All of a sudden, all I could think about was wanting to feel his lips touch mine.

"Justin!" his mother yelled from the kitchen.

We both sat there, frozen. We smiled nervously as he tossed the pillow onto the floor. He jumped up and ran his fingers through his hair, pushing it away from his face, but he kept looking straight into my eyes, prolonging that feeling I had when he was holding my hand.

"Yeah, Mom. What?" he answered.

"I'm going to the store. Could you watch your movie up here, so you can keep an eye on Karl?"

Karl was his crazy little brother.

"I'll be up in a sec!" he said, still looking at me. "Well,

uh . . ."

"I'm going to go," I said. "It's getting late, and I have to go—I mean, get up early." I stumbled over my words, which I'd never done with Justin before. I made my way toward the stairs, feeling like my face was on fire.

"Wait, T. I wanna say something." He hurried up the stairs behind me. But I was out the door before he could say anything. As I walked home in a daze, I wondered what he was going to say. I wondered if I wanted to hear it. It would probably sound something like, "We're friends. We shouldn't jeopardize our friendship."

When I reached my driveway, I thought about what Sacamore had said about opening up. I wondered if what had just happened with Justin counted. I figured it did. Sacamore had said to think about how I felt afterward. Okay, my stomach felt funny, and my hands were shaky. Done with that assignment.

I opened the door to the kitchen and heard the phone ringing. I grabbed it. "Hello?"

My brother, Brian, was on the other end. "Hey, T. What's going on?"

I jumped up and sat on the counter. "Hey, Bri. Nothing really."

"Is Dad around?"

"Uh, I don't know. I just got here," I answered.

"Well, could you find out?" he said.

"Hang on," I said, placing the phone on the counter and hopping down. I walked to the bottom of the stairs and yelled, "Dad!"

No answer.

I jogged back to the phone. "I guess he took Danny somewhere. Pizza probably."

"All right, just tell him I called, okay?"

"No problem," I said.

"Hey, before you go, what's this I hear about you playing baseball?"

Brian, interested in my life? What a shocker. "Who told you that? Dad?"

"No, Danny. He said you're pitching for varsity. Is it true?"

"It's a long story, but it's true."

There was a long pause before he said uncomfortably, "Well, good for you. Just be careful."

I laughed and said, "What, are you getting protective in your old age?"

"Ha, ha, dork. Seriously, there are some real jerks on high school teams."

"Yeah, tell me about it."

"Is Tucker Bratton's little brother on the team? What's his name . . . uh, Rick?"

I felt sick just hearing his name. "Yeah, he is," I said disgustedly. "Why?"

"Eh, Tucker and I got into it a few times. We were always battling over who would start at first base. Plus, his dad played against our dad in college, so I guess there's a little rivalry there. He's not giving you a hard time, is he?"

Besides dating the girl who hates me, turning everyone on

the team against me, and throwing gum into my hair—no, none at all. I considered telling Brian the truth. But I didn't want him to think I was a baby. I was just happy he was talking to me.

"Nah. He's not my favorite person, but he's okay."

"Okay, T. I gotta run. Let me know if you need any advice. 'Cause, you know, I was like the best ball player that school has ever seen."

"Uh-huh, sure. Later, loser."

"Bye, dork."

CHAPTER 11

On Friday, I headed to my weekly therapy session with Sacamore. When I walked into his office, he was sitting at his desk, staring out the window. What a strange guy.

"Hello?" I said.

He turned to look at me and smiled. "Hi, Taylor. I forgot it was Friday."

"Oh, I can leave if you're busy."

"Nice try. Have a seat." As I sat down, he said, "Tell me what's new. How did the homework assignment go?"

I thought back to what had happened in Justin's basement. I wasn't going to say anything about Justin. Besides, Sacamore had said I didn't have to. I stood there for a moment, flushed, and said, "I thought I didn't have to tell you about it."

He rocked back on his chair. "You don't," he answered, "but you just did."

Time to change the subject, I figured, so I scrambled for something else to talk about. "I pitched my first game this week," I said, wondering if that was a good enough diversion from talking about Justin.

"Yes, I know. Do you feel good about that?"

Here we go again with the "how I feel" crap. "It was okay. I didn't lose or win. The score was tied when I stopped pitching, but then the relief pitcher let in some runs, and we lost." I sighed. "No one wants me on the team, though. All the guys hate me. They pretty much ignore me." I was trying to act as if it didn't bother me.

"Does that bother you—that no one's rooting for you?"

"I'm used to it," I answered quickly.

"What do you mean?"

I thought about how nobody at home or at school cared about me or knew I existed, except for Justin and Danny. I started thinking about what had happened at Justin's house the other night. That had given me a bigger thrill than making the varsity baseball team. I was playing on a team where no one cheered for me, a team that tried to pretend I wasn't even there.

"Taylor, what do you mean you're used to it?"

"Mr. Sacamore," I said. "Look at me. I'm just a plain old student. I get average grades. I have bad hair, bad clothes. No one notices me. I made the varsity baseball team, and still no one looks at me in the hall. In fact, most people look away when they see me coming. I'm some sort of a misfit freak."

Sacamore just sat there, waiting for me to keep going. I felt like I was going to cry, but I wouldn't give him the satisfaction. I slumped back in the chair and kicked at my book bag. We sat in silence until the bell rang. Man, this guy pissed me off.

"See you next week," he said as I stormed out the door.

I headed toward the lunchroom. Why did that guy have to make me talk about what a loser I was? How was this helping me? He should've told me how to *not* be a loser. I felt sick to my stomach, so I decided to go out to the courtyard to get some air. When I reached the door, I saw big boobs Stacy and her group of followers, and they were blocking the exit.

"Scuse me," I said, trying to slip by without being noticed. I did *not* feel like dealing with her right now. I was in no mood at all for it.

"There's no excuse for you," she said, laughing with her friends and not moving from the door. "So, I've been meaning to congratulate you on making the varsity baseball team."

I waited, crossing my arms. This ought to be good.

She turned to her friends, giggling. "When you have no mother, I guess you turn into a boy."

I felt my face growing hot. Did she just say my *mother*? I felt a burning pain inside my chest, and I wanted to scream or run or hit something. What did *she* know about my mother? I heard the girls laughing around me. I glared at Stacy. Why *did* my mother leave? Stacy's head was turned toward her friends.

"Stacy, I'm really getting tired of your crap," I said, letting my book bag slide to the floor.

She turned back toward me. "Well, I'm getting tired of you always being around wherever I go. I can't even go to Rick's games without seeing you. Is being on the baseball team your twisted way of finding a boyfriend?"

I started to raise my voice. "If you knew what was good for you, you'd just stop talking," I said as menacingly as I could.

She moved closer to me and jabbed her finger into my shoulder, poking it over and over as she said, "If you knew what was good for you, you'd stay out of my face."

"Get your hands off me," I growled, pushing her arm away from my shoulder.

"Or what, you're going to hit—"

Before she could finish, I swung a hard right toward her made-up face. My fist hit her perfect cheekbone with a loud smack. She screamed and fell to the floor, sniffling and grabbing her face.

"Excuse me," I said calmly, my hands trembling. I grabbed my book bag and darted out the door.

I found refuge on the bleachers at the Little League park. No one else was there, so I sat and stared at the empty field. I wasn't sure how long I'd been sitting there, when I turned to see Justin climbing the bleachers. He sat down beside me and took off his hat.

"Hey," he said.

"Hey."

"Tough day at the office, huh?" he said seriously.

"I guess you heard."

"Oh, *everybody* heard. What in the world happened, T?"

I sighed deeply. "I just couldn't take it any more. Why does that bitch torture me?" I began to get choked up.

Justin moved closer to me and bumped me with his shoulder. "Don't let her bug you. She's just jealous."

"Yeah, right."

"She is. You have the guts to do things she wouldn't do because it doesn't fit into her girlie social world. It's easier to make fun of someone for being different than to be different yourself."

I didn't say anything. He kind of sounded like Sacamore. I knew Justin was trying to make me feel better, and it was sort of working.

"Can I ask you a question, Justin?" I glanced over at him.

"What?"

"Why do you hang out with me?"

"Taylor, what kind of question is that?"

I stared out into the empty field. "Seriously. I mean, I'm a freakin' disaster. I'm not fun to be around. I'm miserable all the time. And all I do is complain. Why would anyone want to be friends with me?"

"You have your happy moments," he said.

"I can't remember the last one. Can you? I think you must enjoy torture or something, spending all this time with me."

I slid back onto the bleachers so my butt was on the footrest. I felt defeated.

Justin slid back to match my posture. "I'll tell you why I hang out with you, T, but I don't want you to think it's pity, 'cause it's not."

"What?" I said. What did he mean by *pity*?

"Well, I don't think you were old enough to remember this," he said, "but I guess I was about seven, and you were about five at the time."

I sat and listened, confused.

Justin continued his story. "We were at one of those block party picnics with all the neighborhood families. It was probably pretty soon after your mom left. Your dad was throwing a baseball with your brother, Brian, and you were watching, waiting for your turn. After a long time waiting, you ran over and picked up the ball they were using. You had the biggest smile on your face, and you were about to throw the ball when your dad stormed over and grabbed it from your hand. He said, 'Taylor, Daddy and Brian are playing.' You were so hurt, you went and sat behind a tree and cried. I remember thinking how messed up that was, even though I was only seven. I felt really bad for you. I walked over and asked if you wanted me to push you on the swings. I put you on a swing and pushed you until you laughed so hard you got the hiccups."

"I don't remember that," I said.

"I do," he said softly.

"So, the reason you're my friend is you feel bad for me 'cause my dad's a jerk?"

"No, that's not why. I knew you'd misunderstand," he said, shaking his head. He took a deep breath. "Listen, the reason I hang out with you is because that day, when I made you laugh, I felt really happy. And I guess I like that feeling. Making you happy makes me feel like I'm on top of the world. I know it's weird, but it's true. I want you to be happy." He reached for my hand. "Can't you be happy, T?"

I sat back up onto the seat and thought about what Justin had just said. He slid back up next to me. "You're crazy," I said. "And why do we keep ending up holding hands?"

"'Cause it makes you smile," he answered. And then it happened—practically in slow motion. He leaned forward and kissed my cheek, and then slowly moved his mouth to kiss mine. And I kissed him back.

It wasn't like striking out a batter, but it was pretty darn close.

CHAPTER 12

When I got home that evening, I started thinking about what Justin had said about my dad. Why was Dad so involved with my older brother all the time and totally annoyed and disgusted with me? He wasn't home from work yet, so I snuck into his room and started poking around. I didn't know what I expected to find, but I needed something to keep the whole Stacy Downbaer incident off my mind. I was sure Dad had gotten a phone call from the school, and I was in deep trouble with him already, so getting caught going through his stuff couldn't make my situation any worse.

I didn't know much about my mom or why she'd left. Dad never talked about it. Brian always said she was never happy, and he figured she'd found something to make her happy, so she left. It was funny. I'd been so mad at my dad for hating me that I wasn't mad at my mother for leaving. I was happy she'd been able to get away from this miserable place. Someday, I'd get away, too.

Digging around in the back of Dad's closet, I came across a photo album I'd never seen before. The only picture I had of my mother was their wedding photo, and in that picture, she was all made-up like a doll, so it was hard to see what she really looked like. I'd always assumed Dad had thrown away all other pictures of her.

I flipped open the album. It seemed to be full of pictures of my mom when she was younger. In many of the photos, she had long, stringy brown hair, just like mine. I knew her parents had died before I was born, and she was an only child. I continued looking at the different shots of her—in a school uniform, blowing out birthday candles . . . and then, I found it—just as my father walked into the room.

"What are you doing in here, young lady?" he demanded.

Stuffing the album under my shirt, I ran to my room and slammed the door, locking it behind me.

He followed me. "Taylor Dresden, open this door! And what is this I hear about a fight at school? Do you know I have to meet with the principal at 7:30 Monday morning about this? Young lady, if you do not open this door, you'll have bigger problems than suspensions."

I opened the door. He was standing there, red in the face, with his hands on his hips. "So what do you have to say about all this?" he said.

"I hit some girl," I answered, looking at the floor.

"Yeah, I heard that part," he said, obviously upset. "For any particular reason?"

All of a sudden, I didn't care any more about making him mad. I wasn't afraid of him. "For the particular reason that she's a bitch." I began to laugh.

He paused, unamused, and took a breath. "Two weeks, no TV, no visits to Justin's. Be waiting in the car at 7:00 Monday morning. Good night." He went into his room and closed the door.

I sat on my bed and pulled out the picture. It was a shot of my mother in a softball uniform. She looked about fifteen years old, and her jersey said "Lowell High School." I turned the picture over. Someone had scribbled "Ellen's first win."

CHAPTER 13

Monday morning was as bad as I had expected. Dad didn't say a word to me on the ride to school. When we got to the vice-principal's office, we had to wait twenty minutes before he called us in—it seemed like years.

"Mr. Dresden?" I finally heard as the vice-principal came out. I watched my father shake his hand. "You and your daughter can step inside now."

I walked into the office and sat in the first empty chair I saw. Sacamore was already sitting in the office, sipping coffee. He introduced himself to my father without saying anything about our Friday sessions.

The vice-principal addressed me first. "So, Taylor, do you have anything to say for yourself?"

How did adults want you to respond to this question? I gave it a shot. "I'm sorry. It won't happen again, but she was saying mean things to me, and I guess I lost my temper."

"We do not tolerate physical violence at this school," he answered. "You will be suspended for two days. I wanted to remove you permanently from the baseball team, but Mr. Sacamore has come to your defense."

My father spoke up. "Sir, if I may interrupt, I think that taking Taylor off the team would be a good idea. Taylor has seemed distracted since this whole baseball thing started. Maybe the team is too much for her to handle."

"But, Dad—"

Mr. Sacamore interrupted my protest. "Mr. Dresden, I've known Taylor for a while, and I don't support removing her from the team. I think baseball, most of the time, keeps her away from negative actions. I believe that some of the girls provoke Taylor. Do you agree, Taylor?"

"I don't know," I mumbled.

"Why don't you tell us what Miss Downbaer said to you that made you so upset." Mr. Sacamore said.

My father looked at his watch—twice.

"She was talking about my mother," I answered.

As he rose, my father looked impatient. "Gentlemen, I'm late for work, unfortunately. I'll take Taylor home to serve her suspension. Are we finished here?"

"If you agree to the terms, Mr. Dresden, they will stand," said the vice principal.

"She made her bed, and now she can lie in it," my dad said.

He didn't even try to defend me.

He dropped me back home, and as he drove away, all he said was, "And don't spend all day watching TV."

I went up to my room, flopped on my bed, and fell asleep. I slept for most of the day. Suspension was great for catching up on sleep. I felt good that Sacamore had stuck up for me today. But I wished it had been my father.

CHAPTER 14

Wednesday morning, I was back at school. For once, I was kind of happy to be there. I hadn't thrown a ball in a week, and I was looking forward to the game after school. I wasn't scheduled to pitch, but I never knew when Coach might put me in to close the game or pitch in relief.

I passed Stacy on the way to my locker, but she didn't look at me. She still had a bruise on her left cheek. I felt kind of guilty about it, but kind of good, too—maybe she'd stop bothering me now.

I entered Sacamore's office a few seconds after the bell rang for first period. I wondered what he'd say about my dad, and waited to thank him for helping keep me on the team. It felt good having something to do after school every day.

"Good morning, Taylor," Sacamore said.

"Hi." I sat down in my usual chair.

"Sorry I pulled you out of class, but I thought we should chat."

"It's okay."

"How were your couple days off?"

"Uh, they were pretty quiet. I just stayed in my room."

"I want to talk about the meeting we had with your father on

Monday morning. Would that be okay with you?"

I shrugged. "I guess so."

"So, tell me about that morning. What were you feeling?"

"I was pretty numb the whole couple of days. It was like I spaced out after the thing with Stacy. I don't remember thinking anything, except . . ." I shifted in my seat.

"Go ahead. What?"

"I wanted to thank you for sticking up for me, Mr. Sacamore. That was nice of you to stick up for me."

He just looked at me and didn't say anything.

"No one ever says anything nice about me," I said. "Teachers always say I'm quiet and I do my work, but that's not really a compliment." I looked at my feet. "What did you think of my father?"

Sacamore leaned forward. "It's not important what I think. I don't have to live with him—you do. What do *you* think of your father?"

I paused for a moment to think what response would satisfy Sacamore and get him to stop prying. But then I realized something. Sacamore wasn't a teacher. He got paid whether he "healed" me or not. He wouldn't repeat what I said to anyone. I was in a place where I could say anything I wanted. No detentions, suspensions, or groundings would be issued. I could probably curse, and Sacamore wouldn't tell. I might as well be honest.

"I think he doesn't care if I live or die." He raised an eyebrow at me, as if to say "enough with the drama, Taylor." I went on. "I just feel like no matter what I do, good or bad, he's mad at me. He's a complete ass, and he sucks as a father."

Sacamore perked up. "You should tell him that."

"What?"

"That he sucks," Sacamore said.

"He already grounded me for two weeks. I don't need to spend the rest of my life in my room," I answered, almost laughing.

Sacamore smiled. "Listen, Taylor, don't tell him in those exact words. Try to be calmer. Tell him you feel he treats you unfairly, and ask him why he does it. You shouldn't be angry with him until you hear his side of the story."

"What do you mean *his side*?"

"Maybe he doesn't think he's being harsh. Maybe something's bothering him. There are two sides to every story. You only know your side. Give him a chance to explain."

"I guess you have a point," I said. The bell was about to ring.

"Good. Let me know on Friday what he says."

"What? I thought we were just talking. I didn't know you were serious!" I stood up in shock.

He stood up and placed his hand on my shoulder. "It couldn't hurt to just talk to him. Now get to class." As I headed for the door, he said, "Taylor, you can do this," and smiled.

For the rest of the day, I thought about what Sacamore had said to me. I was glad when the school day ended because then I could get ready for the game and think about something else.

I had developed a pre-game routine, which I followed whether I was scheduled to pitch or not. I would stop by the cafeteria for a Diet Coke and then stroll down to the locker room. I always chose locker 733 because it was in the back corner and more private. I said "hi" to the softballers and put my bag down on the bench. I enjoyed the fact that the other girls in the locker room had different uniforms from me. It made me feel important. I liked slipping on the long socks and tying my cleats—I always undid the laces and tied them tightly. After wetting my hair, I'd tuck it behind my ears and push my bent hat down on my head. I liked the way my hair stuck out in the back. As I left the locker room, I always grabbed the ledge above the door and did as many pull-ups as I could. I was only up to about nine.

Today's game was at home, so I walked to the field and found a seat in the dugout. Louis Crawley, the guy who usually caught for me, sat next to me. He had the day off, too. He looked around at the other guys before whispering to me.

"Sunflower seeds?" he asked, shoving the bag toward me.

I figured I should say "yes." He was trying to be nice, though I wasn't fond of sunflower seeds. "Sure." I grabbed a handful.

Louis grabbed a handful also and spit the shells on the ground in front of him. I leaned forward, rested my arms on my knees, and joined him in the spitting session. Some of the other guys shook their heads at Louis. I guessed he was breaking some rule—don't feed the girl. But I didn't care. For the first time on this team, I felt a little relaxed.

My thoughts wandered back to my dad. Maybe I should try a different approach with him. Maybe I should just ask him why he hated me.

By the sixth inning, we were down four to three. Jared Lawrence was pitching for us, and he wasn't looking so good. The other team had the bases loaded. I was getting tired of sitting, so I wandered around the dugout while I watched Jared walk in a run.

"Man, five to three," Louis said, shaking his head.

I peeked out of the dugout to look for Justin, but he wasn't there. I hadn't talked to him since that day on the bleachers. My dad wouldn't let me use the phone or leave the house because of my suspension, and I hadn't seen him today at school. I was kind of afraid to see him, though. I thought Justin felt sorry for me that day on the bleachers, and he was trying to make me feel better. I really liked him, though, and the romantic touch to our relationship had been nice while it lasted.

As I went back to the bench to sit down, Coach yelled out, "Dresden, go get warm."

I was shocked. For some reason, I said, "Why?"

Coach looked surprised by my response, but then he laughed. "Because I might put you in. Lawrence's looking finished."

I grabbed my glove and headed up the stairs. Then, I realized I needed a catcher. I stopped and looked at the coach. Was I supposed to ask someone to catch for me?

"Bratton, warm Dresden up, please," he said, as if it were normal—normal to ask Stacy's boyfriend, the guy who hated me, to warm me up. Rick stood up slowly and smugly. He walked even more slowly to the water cooler and got a drink.

"Bratton, did you hear me?" Coach said.

Rick picked up his glove from the bench and, in a snotty voice, said, "Yes, sir." He followed me out of the dugout and down to the bullpen. It wasn't really a bullpen—it was a strip of grass to the side of left field. But I liked to think of it as more than that. I decided it was best to act normal with Rick—to behave as if we always played catch together.

He, however, felt the need to say, "I'm only doing this because Coach told me to. For the record, I can't wait until they bench you permanently or throw you off the team."

I tossed the ball to him and said nothing. I wanted to drop everything and run off the field. But I didn't. I just kept throwing.

"You know, without your curveball, you'd have nothing," Rick said, throwing the ball back to me.

I didn't answer him. I pretended I was throwing at the tree behind my house. And trees didn't talk. A tree couldn't make me cry, even though I felt like crying.

The next few innings went better for us than I'd thought they would. Lawrence didn't allow any more runs, and we scored three runs to put us up 6-5. Louis jogged toward Rick and me. "Taylor," he said, "Coach says you're going in to close."

Rick went back to the dugout. I paced around the strip of grass like a crazy woman. I leaned against the fence and bounced against it. I was going in to pitch the ninth inning. My head felt like it was about to explode. At least we were ahead.

All I had to do was keep it that way.

When it was time to go in, I ran full speed onto the field. I had so much adrenaline pumping through me that I hopped around on the mound and walked around it five times or so.

"Batter up!" the ump yelled.

Great, a lefty.

I stood still and slowly dropped my glove to my waist. I turned my head to look for the catcher's sign, but he was laying his middle finger across his thigh. *What a jerk!* I guessed he wasn't going to help me. I breathed deeply and let my foot move back to begin my delivery. My fingers pushed the smooth ball forward before I released it. The pitch felt perfect as soon as the ball left my fingers.

"Strike one!" the umpire yelled after the tall lanky batter took a big cut. The crowd made a group "Ooo!"

I got the ball back and threw another pitch with barely a pause. It felt like I was in this magical zone, and if I stopped throwing for too long, I might lose my special touch.

"Strike two!"

That was quickly followed by my curve for "Strike three!"

Both of my coaches were standing up in the dugout, watching me as if they knew what I was feeling. Coach Jefferson was patting Perez on the back and smiling from ear to ear.

The next batter swung at the first pitch, and the ball rolled right back to me. I ran forward, scooped it up, and tossed it to first base for out number two. I made eye contact with the first baseman, and he gave me a little thumb's up. I used that small token of encouragement to take down batter number three.

As I threw the final pitch, I felt like I was stuck in slow motion. The batter swung and missed the high fastball, then slammed his bat on the plate in frustration. I stood on the mound and watched everyone else. My own team members on the field jogged past me toward the dugout, kicking up dust. The spectators trickled down from the bleachers like a waterfall. The coaches shook hands and walked back to the dugout. It seemed like everyone else was being quietly sucked away by a vacuum, leaving me alone, as if I'd been on the field by myself the whole time.

By the time I reached the dugout, everyone else was running up the stairs by me to leave. Louis was gone already. No one said, "Nice save, Dresden." I grabbed my bag and walked into the outfield. When I reached the fence by right field, I turned back and stared at the freshly cut grass. I knelt down and ran my hands over the green blades. "Nice save, Dresden," I said aloud and smiled. Whether or not anyone cared about my save, they couldn't take it away from me. I stood up, squeezed through the gap in the fence, and walked with my head held high all the way home.

CHAPTER 15

As I walked home, I thought about confronting my dad. Things had gone so well today on the field, I had to do something to screw up my day.

Sacamore had a point. Maybe I should try to talk to my dad. I hadn't really talked to him since that day I heard him on the phone. What was that? Six years ago? Should I write him a letter? I wasn't good at writing down my thoughts. Having to write essays for school was tough enough. Maybe I should talk to him face-to-face. Yeah, I could do that. After all, how much more could he hate me?

I went up to my room, grabbed a towel, and headed for the bathtub, where I could mull this over. As I soaked my dirty self, I heard Danny run up the stairs, yelling for me.

"What?" I shouted back.

He was out of breath by the time he stopped outside the bathroom door. "Dad's barbecuing! It's the first one of the season, so hurry up!"

Danny was a barbecue freak. It was probably because, when he barbecued, my father actually took the time to cook. And he was pretty good at it. If he was cooking, he must have been in a good mood. Maybe tonight was the right night to talk.

When I got downstairs, the grill was smoking, Danny was

scurrying around setting the outside picnic table, and Dad stood at the grill, flipper in hand. When he saw me, he asked, "Burger or dog, Taylor?"

"Uh, I'll take two dogs," I said, sitting down at the picnic table across from Danny.

"Did you have a game today?" he asked.

"Yeah."

"Did you pitch?"

"I came in as a closer for the last inning."

His mouth was full of potato chips. "You won, right?"

"Six to five," I answered. "I'm starting tomorrow against Mainland."

The grill master made no response. He didn't even look in my direction.

"Cool," Danny said. "I gotta get some more ketchup." He ran into the house.

The three of us sat and ate. Danny and I talked about school and stuff. I tried to avoid the subject of baseball to keep Dad mellowed out. When we finished eating, I told Danny I'd clean up outside, so he could do the dishes left inside. This left just Dad and me together.

As he scrubbed the grill with a wire brush, I tied up the garbage and walked it to the trash can behind the house. I hurried back and sat at the table. Here went nothing.

"Dad, can I talk to you?"

He answered casually, "Yeah, what's up?"

"Maybe you could sit down over here," I asked nervously.

"All right, just let me finish up here." He continued to scrub the grill for a minute or two, then closed the lid and sat down across from me.

"So?" he said, wiping his hands on his apron.

I took a deep breath. "Well, I've been talking to one of the guidance counselors at school, Mr. Sacamore. Remember him from the suspension meeting?"

"Okay, yeah. Why are you meeting with him?"

"He thought it would be a good idea after me hitting Stacy and all."

"Uh-huh."

"So he asked me about my life and stuff at home and you."

Dad just stared.

"And I told him I think you don't like me, and he said maybe I should ask you about it."

"About what?" he said.

"Well," I said softly, "about why you don't like me, Dad."

He quickly got defensive. "What are you talking about, Taylor? Of course I like you. You're my daughter. This is ridiculous." He began to get up.

Trying not to cry, I said, "Wait, please sit. I'm trying to be serious. Maybe it's coming out wrong. I just mean, you don't take much interest in my life or anything I do. You never ask me about school or Justin or baseball. I just want to know why. You talk to the boys about stuff. Why not me?"

Again, he got up from the table. "Taylor, I treat all my kids equally. I'm very busy with work these days, and if you feel ignored, I'm sorry. But I've been busy. I'm the only parent here. Remember?"

I was so angry. He was lying to me. I wanted to yell at him, but instead, I got up slowly, walked toward the back gate, unlatched it, and walked away.

"Where are you going?" he yelled. "It's a school night, and you're still grounded, young lady!"

I didn't answer. I just kept walking.

I was in a fog as I walked aimlessly down the street. I couldn't go to Justin's. It was Wednesday night, and I knew he was at the movies with his mom and brother for "Family Movie Night." We only had "Fight Night" at my house. But I really needed to talk to someone. This was the problem with having only one friend—when he was out, I was out of luck. I guessed I could head toward town, wait until the movie let out, and try to catch Justin as he came out. Bother him as usual with my stupid life. I wondered if Trudy and the softball girls were still at the pizza place. Nah! I didn't know her well enough.

I knew my father would react that way—deny everything. But I was still pissed. Maybe I should keep walking and never go back. Would he even notice?

I continued walking past the theater and turned onto a side street, when I heard a loud, deep, "Dresden!" coming from someone's porch.

I looked up and saw half the baseball team sitting on the porch, drinks waving in the air. "It's Dresden. Do the wave." They all stood up and sat down, yelling "Woo hoo!"

I stopped and smiled. I wasn't sure if they were being nice or mocking me, so I waved and kept walking.

"Dresden, where you going? Come on up and hang out," yelled Tony Lighton, who played first base.

"No thanks, guys," I answered.

They began to chant, "Dresden, Dresden."

Tony tried again. "Come on, we'll be nice. It's only the six of us."

I didn't see Rick or any of the Stacy crowd. And Tony had given me that tiny thumbs-up after the game. Also, I saw Louis, who I knew was cool with me. And where else was I going anyway? What the heck. I headed up the driveway toward the house.

Once I reached the porch, I could tell they didn't know what to do with me. I was sure they didn't think I'd actually join the party. Tony offered me a beer. It was his house, and his parents were in the Bahamas for the week. I took the cup, just so I would have something to hold, and sat down on the porch. I held it tightly in my hand, but I couldn't bring myself to take a sip. I brought it up to my mouth, but the smell made me feel like puking. The last time I'd touched beer, I ended up in such a mess, I was afraid of what might happen this time. Plus, I had to be on guard in case anyone here was planning something to humiliate me.

They were actually pretty nice to me. We talked about our win today and how we were facing Mainland tomorrow and how tough they were. Before I knew it, I was starting to relax. That's when the rest of the team started arriving.

When someone's parents are away, word gets around quickly. A group of guys I recognized from our team showed up. Some of them were carrying book bags that definitely did not have books in them. They slapped hands with Tony and said some of the girls would be over in a little while. They went to the kitchen and started raiding the fridge and the cabinets, pulling out bags of chips and pretzels. Someone turned on music and opened the front windows to let the sound out. I sat there quietly, trying to be invisible.

Rick had come in with this group of guys. He looked over at me and nodded to the other guys. "Ah, the pitcher's here," he said. He then took a sip of beer and headed inside.

I wasn't sure if that was a good or bad comment, but I definitely felt like I'd overstayed my welcome. I tried to figure out how to make a quick exit. All I needed was a bunch of giggling girls, or worse, Stacy herself, to arrive. I got up and started moving to the edge of the porch.

"You leaving, Dresden?" Louis asked, blocking me with his leg.

"Yeah, I should get going," I said, thinking that was enough explanation.

"Aw, come on," Louis said. "Hang out for a while, so I have someone to talk to. Pitchers and catchers have to bond, you know."

Louis was a really nice guy. The other guys picked on him because he was kind of chubby. I figured he was being sincere, but I had to go.

I made up an excuse. "I'm meeting someone at the movies, and I'm already late. Sorry."

He shrugged. "Okay. I'll see ya later."

I was already halfway down the sidewalk when I saw them—Stacy and her two disciples, Rhonda and Tali. They were chatting and laughing until Tali saw me, tapped Stacy, and pointed toward me. All three stopped dead in their tracks. Stacy yelled to Rick, who was now on the front porch, "Rick, why is *she* here?"

"Not my house, Stace," he answered.

"I was just leaving," I said, moving around them.

"Good," Stacy said firmly. "Crawl back into your hole."

I stopped walking away from them. And then, I paused to think, which is not something I normally do—I usually just react. What would Sacamore say in this situation? Probably something like, "The more you hurt others, the more you hurt yourself." Or he'd say, "Try to see it from her side." *Her side?* Maybe she was afraid of me. After all, I did get her good last time. Maybe she felt threatened by me hanging out with her crowd. Maybe this crowd was all she had. Sacamore would also say, "Talk it out, Taylor."

I turned back toward the three girls and spoke calmly. "You know, Stacy, you probably think a lot of girls envy you. But I feel sorry for you . . ." I paused and swallowed. My throat was dry. ".

. . because I believe that what goes around comes around. And if you keep being a cruel bitch to everyone, one day, when high school is over, and you're not in this tiny world that you think is reality, someone's going to give it right back to you."

"Oh, like I'm so scared," she said to her cronies.

I took one step toward her and raised my fist. She flinched and backed up.

I smiled, turned, and walked away. When I got home, I walked through the front door and saw my father reading in the living room. He looked up at me briefly, and I looked at him. We said nothing. He went back to his book, and I went upstairs to bed.

CHAPTER 16

On Thursday, the day of our next game, the hours seemed to drag by. I was in History class, staring out into the hallway, when I saw Justin walk by the classroom door. Then, I saw him go by again. Mr. Krimick was droning on about the Civil War. "Yes, this will be on the test," he kept saying. Justin was again at the door, and he knocked twice. Mr. Krimick yelled for him to enter.

Justin stuck his head inside the door. "Excuse me, Mr. Krimick, but they need to see Taylor Dresden in the office."

Mr. Krimick nodded toward me. "Taylor, better take your things. The bell's about to ring."

I scooped up my books and quickly left the room. Justin was already halfway down the hall, laughing and beckoning to me. "Come on!"

I caught up with him. "Where are we going?"

"It's lunch time. I thought we'd go someplace nice."

"Justin, lunch isn't for an hour. We'll miss fourth period."

He stopped. "Don't worry," he said. "I got everything covered. My buddy Jack's going to tell Ms. Miller you're at the nurse's, puking and stuff."

I thought a minute. "All right, but I have to be back by last period or they won't let me pitch today."

We hurried out one of the side doors and snuck quickly through the parking lot. Justin headed into the woods behind the school, and I followed. I knew kids always came out here to smoke and fool around when they cut class, but I'd never been out here.

We walked for a while, and then we came to a clearing by a little stream. Justin sat down on a fallen log and opened his backpack. He pulled out two deli sandwiches.

"Turkey or roast beef?" he asked.

I sat down next to him. I wasn't hungry at all, just curious. But I said, "I'll take the turkey."

He handed me the sub and a bottle of iced tea. While he began devouring his sandwich, I just sipped the iced tea and looked at the stream. After he'd eaten half his food, he took a big gulp of soda and turned toward me, wiping his hands on his jeans. "So, I guess this thing with you and me is a bust, huh?"

"What?" I said, surprised.

He twisted his bottle cap back on. "Well, ever since that day on the bleachers, you haven't talked to me, so I figured you're not interested."

I was confused. "Justin, that's not it. I've just been busy with baseball. And crap with my dad and Sacamore—"

He interrupted. "T, it's okay. You don't need to make excuses. I just brought you out here to tell you you're off the hook. It's cool if you're not looking for a relationship. We can just be buds like we've always been."

I was speechless. Of course I liked him. What was he talking about—*let me off the hook*? Maybe he wanted out, and he was turning it around on me. I wasn't sure what to say. I just sat there stupefied, looking at the ground. I wasn't going to tell him I was interested if he was looking for a way to just be friends again. I didn't want to lose him as a friend. Our friendship had been the only thing that kept me from jumping off a cliff these past few years.

Justin spoke again. "So we're still friends, right?"

I nodded and said softly, "Of course we're still friends . . . if that's what you want."

"Good, I feel better." He began eating again. "So, who are you pitching against today?"

I answered all his questions about the game. We were playing against Mainland, and I was starting. They had a serious power hitter, Tommy Bucci. Yes, I was nervous. But as I spoke, all I could think about was what had just happened. I hadn't wanted a boyfriend before all this stuff happened, but now was I supposed to go back to not kissing him? Go back to not thinking about kissing him? I couldn't stand the thought. Maybe I should just tell him how I felt.

"I guess we should start heading back," Justin said.

We made our way back to school. And, like an idiot, I said nothing.

I was not in the mood for baseball that afternoon. I downed

a soda before the game, trying to wake myself from the coma I'd been in since lunch. I stumbled out of the locker room. I hated pitching home games. I actually felt more support from the crowd at away games. I didn't expect them to cheer for me, so their silence made sense and felt right. At home, the silence was uncomfortable. Even if someone wanted to cheer for me, they probably would've been made an outcast for doing so. This morning, I'd been looking forward to pitching, especially after my save yesterday, but I wasn't excited now. I'd lost my game face. I trudged down the hall, toward the back door of the school.

When I rounded the corner by the trophy case, I was hanging my head so low, I ran right into Mr. Sacamore.

"Ooh, sorry about that," I said before realizing who I'd run into. Then I looked up. "Oh, hey, Mr. Sacamore."

"Taylor, this *is* a coincidence," he said, placing his hand on my shoulder. "You okay?" He looked me in the eyes.

"Sure, I guess," I said, shrugging.

"You want to talk? I have some time."

I looked out the door at the end of the hall and saw the guys warming up. "Uh, I can't right now. I don't have time. I'm starting today."

"If something's on your mind, you better clear it up before you get on the field."

I looked at Sacamore. I looked outside. I thought about my dad and about Justin. I dropped my head and felt the tears well up in my eyes. What was I thinking? I couldn't pitch right now. I stammered, "I just . . . I just can't do this any more. I can't do any of this. Everyone hates me."

I turned, walked quickly in the other direction, and pulled my hat down so no one would see the water works that were about to start. I pushed open the gym door. It was empty, thank God. The bleachers were pulled out for the teacher vs. student volleyball game scheduled for later. I ducked behind the bleachers and walked under the dark wood until I was out of sight. I sat down against the wall.

I was so numb, I couldn't get the tears to come out. I would hide in here, I decided, and somebody else would have to pitch. To my right, I heard the sound of the gym door creaking open. Shoot—Sacamore. Maybe he wouldn't find me.

"Taylor?" he said in a loud whisper. "You in here?" He walked toward the center of the gym. As he neared the other end of the bleachers, my eyes followed the sound of his footsteps. The waxed gym floor squeaked when he stopped to peek under the bleachers. He smiled when he saw me.

I was actually relieved he found me. I was such a sucker. I was really starting to like Sacamore. He seemed to truly like me, and that was something I needed. Carefully ducking his head, he stepped over the metal frame of the bleachers. He settled himself next to me and opened the water bottle he was carrying. Pointing to the bottle, he offered me a sip, but I shook my head. He sighed. We just sat there.

Finally, he said, "I'm going to tell you a secret, Taylor."

I turned my hat backwards and faced him, waiting.

"It doesn't matter who likes you. There are always going to

be people who don't like you. Heck, there are even people who don't like me." He snorted out a laugh. "What matters most is that you like yourself."

"What's to like?" I said glumly.

He got to his feet but stayed bent over so he wouldn't hit his head. "Well, that's something you have to figure out yourself. Now, I believe you have a game to pitch." He began to walk away, but he turned back to say, "I'll tell you one thing I like about you—you're not a quitter. You haven't given up on fixing things with your dad, and you haven't given up on this team yet, either." He spoke firmly but seemed a bit disappointed. I didn't want Sacamore to hate me, too.

And with those words, something took over my body like magic. I stood up and headed outside.

Because of my detour under the bleachers, I was late getting out to the field, so I had little time to warm up. Jamie London was catching for me today. I always felt like he threw the ball extra hard back to me, just to be a macho jerk. He hardly ever gave me signs on what to throw. He didn't care about winning—he just cared about his own batting average.

I jogged out to the mound for the first inning. I kicked at the rubber, cleared the dirt off it, kicked it again, and cleared more dirt off, trying to focus.

"Batter up!" the ump yelled.

Not only was I feeling horrible, but I was armed and dangerous. The first batter was nearly beheaded by the high fastballs I was hurling. I walked him on four straight pitches. The next batter took one on the shin and was awarded first base. Great. Two on, no outs. Now the crowd was getting interested.

"Take her out, Perez!" a fan yelled.

"She's gonna kill somebody!" another parent screamed.

But Perez left me in. Before facing the next batter, I paced around. *Stop thinking about Justin. Stop thinking about Dad.* I looked for Justin in the crowd. He wasn't there. Nobody was ever there for me.

I wound up and delivered the ball. I'd never thrown so hard before. It was like all my anger was in that ball. It flew way over London's head, forcing the umpire to duck, and slammed into the fence. It didn't fall to the ground, but lodged itself in the mesh wire. Both runners advanced because of the wild pitch.

"What the . . ." I heard from the crowd.

The umpire walked toward the ball and examined it like it was a rare fossil. He waved for Perez to come out of the dugout.

"This girl is too wild, Coach. I think you should consider taking her out," the umpire said. Perez headed toward me on the mound.

"I'm not taking you out, Dresden. I refuse to take anyone out in the first inning. I'm just out here to humor the umpire. Get it together, and get out of the inning," he said, and then jogged back to the dugout. He gave the umpire a big thumbs-up. The ball was still stuck in the fence, so the ump threw me a new one.

I tried to push away my feelings so I could focus on pitching. *Just get the ball over the plate. Relax, and get it over the plate.* The next batter made contact, and his weak pop-up was easily caught by our shortstop, holding the runners on second and third. Thank goodness! At least we had one out now. I was breathing hard. The next two batters grounded out to end the inning. Phew, that was close. At least they hadn't scored . . . yet. I hurried back to the dugout to hide.

As I rounded the fence, I saw Sacamore standing on the other side of it, looking concerned. *Great, not again.* He waved me over to him.

"Taylor, relax out there," he said, his fingers sticking through the chain link fence.

I shrugged. "I can't stop thinking about stuff," I said. "It's messing me up."

"What stuff? Did you talk to your dad?"

"Yeah, that was a disaster. And now Justin is blowing me off or something. I can't do anything right."

"Taylor, there was more to that secret I started telling you about under the bleachers. No matter what else is going on, you have to remember that you're good at baseball. You're a great athlete. Maybe nobody has ever told you that before, but it's the absolute truth. If this is the only thing you think you have going for you, then use it. Put all your positive energy into pitching. Make it your passion, and everything else will fall into place."

I thought about what Sacamore was saying, and I smiled. No one had ever told me I was good. He had a point. I *was* pretty good. But today, I was destroying myself out there. But just because everything else was going wrong didn't mean baseball had to go wrong, too.

I sat down on the bench, slipped my jacket onto my right arm to keep it warm, and put my head on my hands. I sat there, trying to breathe and relax. It was usually considered bad luck to talk to the pitcher between innings, but to me, at that moment, Sacamore's talk was the good luck I needed. I sat there and tried to think about nothing except getting the ball in the strike zone. "Just pitch," I told myself. "Just pitch."

I heard the scuffling of feet around me, and I knew it was the second inning. Jamie tapped me on my leg with his glove—his way of saying "It's time." After adjusting my hat and tossing my jacket on the bench, I jogged confidently to the mound. I had found the focus I'd always needed.

I threw the next inning as if there was a string going from my arm to Jamie's glove. A whole series of perfect strikes—three batters up, three batters down.

The next innings went just as quickly. I didn't let anyone get on base. In the sixth inning, my arm was starting to feel like mush. I got two quick groundouts, and then I walked a guy. I struck out the next batter for the third out, making my strike-out total for the game ten batters. As I hustled back to the dugout, I heard it. A small section of the crowd was clapping. I looked up and saw the top row of the bleachers standing up and clapping softly. There were some boys, girls, and parents standing there. I didn't recognize any of them, but they were cheering for me. Before I reached the dugout, I tipped my hat just a little to thank them. They had no idea how much it meant to me. A smile stretched across my face. I didn't care about looking tough in front of the team. I let myself feel good for once.

Perez took me out after that inning, which was fine with me. He was always afraid I'd throw my arm out. I sat on the bench, spitting sunflower seeds with Louis, happy as a pig in slop.

Louis turned to me after a while. "Dresden," he said quietly, "nice pitching out there."

I nodded, spit, and simply said, "Thanks." But inside, I was doing cartwheels. Tony walked by, stuck his hand out, and gave me a quiet low five, so only Louis and I could see.

We won the game 6-0. It was my first win, and my first shut-out. After the game ended, I headed back to the locker room to collect my stuff. I actually held my head high as I walked back toward the building. I wanted to find Sacamore and hug him, to thank him for giving me a chance. Instead, I ran through the halls like a crazy girl, banging my glove against the long row of lockers and jumping up to smack the lights. Winning wasn't everything, but it definitely was something!

The locker room was buzzing. The softball team had won by ten runs, and all the girls were dancing to the radio in celebration. I walked in and had to laugh. Trudy was standing on the benches with Denise Rodriguez, singing at the top of her lungs.

"Hey, Taylor!" Trudy said. "I heard you guys won, too! Congratulations!"

"Thanks. Same to you guys," I said.

"We rule!" Denise screamed as she jumped down and skipped toward the showers.

"You're coming across the street to celebrate with us today, right Taylor?" Trudy said, giving me a friendly tap on the arm.

I was so high from the win, I said, "Sure. I could eat some pizza." And I actually went.

When I got to the pizza place, all the girls were squished into two booths in the corner, downing slices of pizza. Trudy and Denise waved me over.

"Taylor, back here!" Trudy yelled. She was always so chipper.

"Hey, Trudy," I said, squeezing in next to her.

"Help yourself," she said, shoving a paper plate toward me.

I folded the pizza in half and took a bite. We ate pizza all the time at home, but it never tasted as good as this.

"So, I've got a good trivia question for everyone," Trudy said.

"Okay, go," one girl said.

"What pitcher has the most career wins?"

Everyone started yelling out names. "Ryan."

"Johnson!"

"Are you talking about softball or baseball?" I asked.

Trudy laughed. "Oh yeah, like there are so many famous softball teams. Baseball, silly."

I held up my hands as if to say "duh." I knew the answer. "Oh. Well then, Cy Young."

"Ding, ding! You win!" she said. She proceeded to take an

ice cube from her drink and put it down the back of my shirt.

"Oh, you little . . ." I said, reaching into my own glass and flinging a cube her way. A few other girls followed suit by grabbing for ice.

"Hey, knock it off!" yelled the man behind the counter. "You girls can finish your food outside!"

We were all cracking up as we grabbed the pizza box and ran out of the restaurant.

Still laughing, I said to Trudy and Denise, "I should get going."

"Here," Trudy said, reaching into her purse for a pen. "Give me a call. We might see a movie or something on Saturday, and you can come." She wrote her number on a napkin and handed it to me.

"Uh, okay," I said. "See you guys."

CHAPTER 17

The next morning, I hurried to Bio class, suddenly remembering we had a test on that stupid dead pig. I had let my lab partner do all the dissecting, and all I knew about the pig was that it smelled like vomit. The hall was packed with people rushing to class, and I was trying to maneuver my way through the crowd. I bumped into a few people, and then I found myself face-to-face with Justin.

"Hey!" he said enthusiastically.

I was still rushing forward but said, "Hey, I got a test."

"OK, talk to you later. I heard you had a good game," he yelled as I reached the stairs.

I waved and ran up the stairs. When I got to Bio and had the test in front of me, I finally had time to think. I answered everything I knew in about ten minutes, so I had time to relax and pretend I was thinking about dead pigs. That had been a bad way to see Justin. He probably thought I was ignoring him. This getting-to-class-on-time thing really interfered with my social life. Maybe I should write him a letter about what was going on. Yeah, right—a letter? What was I thinking?

Before I knew it, the bell was ringing. I tossed my test with the others onto Mr. Dewey's desk and then walked to Algebra class, still thinking about Justin.

Later that day, which was a Friday, I headed to Sacamore's office, as usual. Maybe I'd experienced a "breakthrough" when he talked to me by the dugout. I'd begun to believe in myself, and it had worked. I remembered the good feeling I had after really putting my heart into the game.

I knocked on his door and slowly opened it. He was sitting at his desk, scribbling something.

"Hey," he said casually. "Big T . . . Come on in, sister."

I still thought he was a weirdo, though I was starting to like his hokey greetings. He made me feel as if there were more good guys out there besides Justin Kennedy. I sat down on the couch and put my feet up on the coffee table. I sighed, thinking of Justin.

"Why the sigh, Ms. Dresden?" Sacamore asked, looking up from his paperwork.

I'd never really told him about Justin. I'd said we were friends and all, but I'd never told him about the relationship stuff. Sacamore *did* help me with the baseball thing, though. Maybe he could help me with Justin. I figured I'd give it a shot.

"Remember at the game, when I mentioned Justin?" I asked.

"I recall that," he said, nodding.

"Well, we were always friends, and I thought we were getting more serious than that. And then he told me it was okay if we were just friends."

"You don't want to be friends?"

"No, I do. That's not what I mean . . ."

"You mean, you want to be more than friends?" Sacamore asked.

"Yeah, I think so."

"But he doesn't?"

"He doesn't *what*?" I was getting confused.

"Want to be more than friends?"

"Well, I think he did, but he thought I didn't, so he said he'd let me off the hook and we could just be friends."

"Uh-huh," Sacamore said. "I'm completely confused."

"Yeah, join the club," I said.

We both began to laugh. It felt really good to laugh—it wasn't something I did a lot. I looked at Sacamore as he was laughing. His eyes squinted shut, and his dimples showed through his five o' clock shadow. At that moment, I believed he truly cared about helping me.

Sacamore sucked back the laughter and gave a typical therapist solution. "Well, Taylor, as I always say, if you have a problem with someone, the only way to remedy it is to talk it over with them and be honest about your feelings. If you like this guy, tell him. What bad could come of it? He said you'd always be friends."

"Yeah, I know. We could always talk, but it seems harder now. And the last time I tried your talking thing, it wasn't exactly successful."

"You mean with your father?"

"Yeah."

"Would you share with me what happened with him?"

I shrugged. "I tried to ask him straight out why he didn't like me, and he denied it. He said he was a busy man and I was being silly."

"Go on."

"He got pissed and said he was the only parent around, if I hadn't noticed," I said, mimicking him sarcastically.

Sacamore perked up when he heard that. "That's it, Taylor."

"What?"

"He answered your question."

"He did?" I asked.

"Yes. He let you know he's upset about being the only parent."

I put up my hands and asked, "How's that telling me why he doesn't like me?"

"Because it doesn't sound like he's angry with *you*. It sounds like he's angry with your mother."

My mother? I'd never thought about him being mad at *her*. I always thought he was glad she was gone. I thought he'd wanted her to leave. He never acted like he missed her.

"You think so?" I asked.

"Could be."

"But that doesn't explain why he treats me like garbage," I said, still confused.

"No, but it should show you he has other things on his mind, just as you have other things on yours, like Stacy, school, baseball . . . He may not realize he's ignoring you. Just as you may not have realized you were ignoring Justin with all those other things on your mind."

"I wasn't ignoring Justin," I said defensively.

"Does he know that? Does he know how you feel about him?"

"No, not exactly . . . but he knows I care," I said softly.

"Are you sure? It's a two-way street, Taylor. Your father may think he's sending you the message that he cares, but he's so preoccupied with other things that the message isn't coming across clearly."

Wow. This guy was making a lot of sense—but maybe too much all at one time. "Whoa," I said, "information overload."

He smiled. "Pretty heavy stuff, huh?"

"You said it," I answered.

He glanced up at the clock. Our time was almost up. "So listen, Taylor. When you leave here today, just remember one thing."

"What's that?"

"Remember that we all have our own problems. If someone hurts you, it may not be intentional. They may just be thinking of something else."

"I got it, Mr. Sacamore," I said, moving toward the door.

"Good luck with Justin," he said. "And don't give up on your dad."

After practice, Justin's skater friends and I were hanging

out in Justin's basement, playing video games and eating all the junk food we could find. I was sitting on the couch, flipping through an issue of *Sports Illustrated*. I wished everyone would leave so I could have a chance to tell Justin how I really felt. Everybody except Tommy and me had gone upstairs to get more snacks.

Tommy slapped the magazine out of my hand as he sat down next to me. "You're such a jock, Taylor."

I wacked him with the magazine. "Jerk," I said, pretending to be pissed.

"Oh, you wanna mess with me?" he said.

"I'll drop you like yesterday's trash," I answered, making a fist.

"That's it. It's on!' He jumped up and started doing his Muhammad Ali impression. "You see the footwork I got going on here, baseball girl? Huh? You're going down." His shorts were so baggy, his legs looked like pencils hopping around.

I started laughing. He jumped on me and pretended to punch me in the head. I couldn't stop laughing. "Knock it off, chicken legs!" I yelled. He flipped me over and sat on my back.

"What you gonna do now, tough girl?"

I picked up the magazine. "Read," I said.

He picked me up again, so I was hovering above the couch. "Here comes the body slam!" he said, dropping me to the couch, then falling on top of me. We were both laughing. As we untangled, he asked, "You and Justin aren't a thing, right?"

I didn't want anyone else to know about our business, so I

said, "No. Why would you think that?"

"No reason," he answered, and then he stared at me for a minute.

"What?" I said.

And then he kissed me on the cheek. "Want to go out to my car and fool around?" he said, just as Justin was coming down the stairs. Stunned, I didn't move a muscle. Then I quickly wiggled to a sitting position, and Tommy moved back toward the video game, trying to act natural. But I knew Justin had seen us. He stopped at the bottom of the stairs for a minute, put down the bag of chips on the side table, and said, "I gotta make a call. I'll be back." He hustled up the stairs.

"Shoot," I said and ran up after him.

"I thought you guys weren't together!" Tommy yelled behind me.

I got up to the kitchen in record time, but Justin wasn't there. Ray was staring into the fridge. "Where's Justin?" I asked.

"Uh . . ." Ray looked up, thinking. "He said he needed some air or something. He took my car." He laughed and added, "Sounded like something my dad would say—'need some air.'"

I pushed open the screen door, but Justin was gone. I wasn't going to give up on him. I'd talk to him later when we got a chance to be alone.

CHAPTER 18

When I arrived home from Justin's house that afternoon, I saw a strange car in the driveway. I went around to the back kitchen door and heard a familiar voice. Turns out my brother, Brian, was home from college. I wondered what was up. He still had a few weeks before finals. Even during the summer, when he had no classes, he usually stayed with his buddies at the shore. He rarely came home.

I walked into the kitchen and saw Brian standing by the oven with his arms folded. Some girl was perched on a stool, leaning on the counter. Brian sighed and said quietly, "Hey, Taylor."

I could tell something was wrong. Normally, he'd just call me a dork and smack me in the head as a greeting. "What are you doing home?" I asked.

"This is Lori," he said, nodding toward the girl on the stool.

"Hi," I said.

Brian moved to the counter and said, "T, I have some bad news, but I don't want you to get upset."

I stood there, waiting for the rest.

"Let me start by saying he's okay and everything, but Dad's been in a little car accident."

I felt like I was going to throw up. "What? Where is he?"

"Relax. He's at the hospital—St. Mary's. He's got a broken

arm and a concussion, so they're keeping him overnight for observation. But I'm here, so you guys don't need to worry."

I put down my book bag and sat down on a stool. I was waiting to see how I felt. Dad was hurt? In a car accident? So when I was talking about him with Sacamore earlier in the day, he was probably lying on the road or getting put in an ambulance. I imagined what it might've been like. He was bleeding, and the paramedics were saying, "Sir, can you hear me?" They were going through his wallet, trying to find out who he was. The nurse was sticking tubes in him and saying, "Contact the family." While he was going through all that, I was complaining about him. Sacamore was right. I never thought about anyone but myself.

"T," I heard Brian say. "You okay?"

I snapped out of my trance. "Yeah. Can we go see him?"

"I was waiting for Danny to get home, and then we'll all go."

I jumped off the stool. "I'm gonna go now. I'll take my bike over there."

"You sure, honey?" the Lori girl said. "We have my car."

But I was already at the back door. "I'll see you there."

I pedaled as fast as I could toward the hospital. I knew Brian had said Dad was okay, but I felt like I had to see for myself. I kept thinking about what Dad had said after our barbecue. He was the only parent I had, even if he *was* a crappy one.

It was beginning to rain, and I was beginning to cry. My tears mixed with the raindrops and made a trail along my cheek before being swept away by the wind.

When I reached the hospital, I was sweating but cold. I dumped my bike on the grass and went in through the emergency room entrance. Instead of asking anyone where he was, I darted down a long hall, peeking inside rooms to look for him. The hospital wasn't that big, so I was sure I'd find him. And I did. I passed the elevator doors, and then I saw him. He was in the last room. The door was wide open, so I could see Dad lying in bed. His arm was in a sling across his chest. An old man was sleeping in the bed next to him. When I stepped into the room, Dad opened his eyes.

"Taylor, hey," he said slowly. "Are the boys here?"

I stood very still. "They're coming soon," I said.

He propped himself up on the pillows and said, "Well, don't worry. I'm fine. They're just going to keep me overnight for observation. Brian will get you guys dinner and everything."

He was so calm and matter-of-fact. I was standing there, wet and shaking, looking him over and wanting to hug him. But all I did was reach out and touch his broken arm. I stared at my hand as I touched his arm, as if his arm would break again if I pushed too hard.

Dad seemed uncomfortable with me touching him. He patted my hand and tried to make light of the situation. "I'm fine, Taylor. Go on home and get something to eat."

I pulled my hand away and backed up until I hit a chair that was against the wall. I sat down and said, "I'll wait for Brian." I searched for a reason to stay and watch him. "It's raining. I can't ride my bike, 'cause it's raining," I stuttered. I didn't know why, but I just had to stay. I guessed he realized he'd have to put up with me for a while, so he closed his eyes and sighed.

"I'm just going to rest my eyes for a few minutes," he said, laying his head back on the pillows.

I watched him closely from my chair. He looked tired, and his hair, from lying on it, was pushed up on one side. I'd never seen my father look helpless before. He needed a mother right now . . . or a wife.

After a while, I walked to the side table and poured him a glass of ice water. "Here, Dad, have a drink," I said, sitting on the edge of the bed.

He pulled himself up a bit. "Thanks, sweetheart," he said groggily. He took a sip and then slipped back to sleep. He'd never called me "sweetheart" before.

I sat in the chair for at least an hour until the boys arrived. While waiting, I replayed the last few months in my mind. I thought about how the only times I'd spoken to Dad in the past few months were when we fought. I always felt horrible after we fought. I shouldn't hate my father. People said there was a fine line between love and hate, and I guessed that was true. I didn't actually hate him. I just wanted him to like me, so when he ignored me, it made me mad. I'd never had anyone tell me I was good at things. No one had ever hung my report card or a picture I'd drawn on the fridge. I just wanted one picture of my dad, smiling and proud, with his arm around me. I knew he cared about me. He had to. I was his daughter. When he got better, I decided, I'd be nice to him, no matter how he treated me.

Finally, Brian came into the room with Lori, followed by Danny. Brian went over to the bed and nudged Dad. "Pop, you okay?" he asked.

Dad sat up. "Hey, guys," he said. "Yeah, I'm fine."

Brian shouted, "The doctor says they're letting you out of here tomorrow." Why was he shouting? Dad hadn't lost his hearing, had he? Still shouting, Brian said, "I'm going to pick up a pizza and take the kids home, okay? Do you need anything?"

Dad shook his head. "No, you guys go on home."

We all said goodbye and left the hospital. We piled into the car and drove to Tony's Trattoria for dinner. I took about three bites of the pizza and felt sick. The Lori girl kept trying to talk to me, asking me about school and boys. I didn't answer.

Danny spoke up for me after a while. "Taylor plays baseball," he said. "She's a pitcher."

That shut her up. I guess she didn't know how to talk to a girl who played baseball. I was happy for the silence, but wished Justin were here. I needed to talk to him before something happened to him and I lost my chance. I got up from the table and said, "I've got to make a phone call." Brian looked up. "You want my cell phone?"

"It's kind of personal," I answered shyly.

"Well, take it outside," he said, reaching into his pocket and fishing out his phone. "Don't wander too far."

I took the phone and walked outside. I dialed Justin's house, and his mother answered. I asked for Justin, and then a few moments later, he got on the phone.

"Hi, it's Taylor," I said.

He answered quietly, "T, what's up?"

"I really need to talk to you. Can you meet me at my house in like a half hour?"

"T, we already talked," he said, sounding defeated. "It's all good."

I knew he was going to say that, so I used my situation to my advantage. "No, Justin . . . My dad's been in a car accident, and I could use some company."

"Crap, Taylor. Is he okay?"

"Yeah, he's going to spend the night in the hospital. So could you meet me?"

"I'll be there. Half hour?"

"Yeah, thanks."

"Hang tight," he said and hung up.

When we got home, I headed upstairs to my room. I figured Justin wasn't coming for a while, if he was coming at all. No, he was coming. He was the one person I could count on. I flopped on the bed, stared at the ceiling, and zoned out for a while.

I thought about the game yesterday, striking out ten batters. Man, that was a rush. I hadn't felt a surge of power like that since I threw those bricks through the school windows. I definitely liked striking guys out and throwing with all my might. It was better than breaking windows, and easier than talking to people.

There was a tap on the door. "You in here?" Justin asked.

I sat up fast and smiled. "Yeah."

He walked over and sat on the bed. "How's your dad?"

"They said he's got to stay overnight. He's got a concussion and a broken arm."

"You handling it okay?" he asked, concerned.

I nodded my head. "Yeah, I think he'll be fine."

We sat in silence for a while. Then Justin said, "You want to listen to a CD to get your mind off it? I've got a few new bands in my book bag."

I looked at him and said slowly, "I didn't ask you over to talk about my dad . . . I wanted to talk about us. And what happened in your basement this afternoon."

"Taylor, it's no big deal. We're just friends, remember? If you're interested in Tommy, that's cool with—"

"Justin," I said, cutting him off, "I'm not interested in Tommy. That was just a misunderstanding."

"It looked like you were having fun with him."

"We were just wrestling, and then I guess he thought it was something more." I paused and took a breath. "He caught me completely off guard. After you left, I told him I wasn't into him. I swear."

Justin looked relieved. He sat quietly for a minute and then said, "Thank God. I mean, if you're going to go with someone, you could do a lot better than Tommy."

"I thought you guys were friends," I said.

"Oh, Tommy's my friend, but he's an idiot." Justin laughed. "Remember the time he took that test in Geography class and wrote that the capital of New Jersey was New York?"

I smiled. "But that was a long time ago."

"Nope. He was still in ninth grade then!"

We both laughed. It felt good to be laughing with Justin again.

"Thanks for clearing that up about Tommy," he said. "I feel better now."

"Well, there's more," I said, eager to get on with it.

He kicked off his shoes and pulled himself up on the bed, leaning on one elbow. "Let me get comfortable first," he said, teasing me.

I took a deep breath. "OK, well the thing is, when we had that talk in the woods, I felt like you misunderstood what I was thinking about you. You thought I didn't want to be more than friends, but that's not exactly true."

He looked confused. "It's not?" he said.

"No. I guess I was just preoccupied with baseball and my dad and getting suspended and all that stuff, and I kind of forgot to tell you how I was feeling."

"So how *were* you feeling?"

"Uh, I was feeling good. Happy, I guess. That day, after I hit Stacy and you told me all those things on the bleachers, I was freaked out, but in a good way."

"But you never talked to me after that," Justin said. "It was like you wanted to pretend it didn't happen or something."

"No, that's not it. I couldn't stop thinking about it. I didn't know how to react . . . I've never had anyone like me before."

"Come on, Taylor."

"Seriously." I hesitated. "No one ever kissed me before," I said.

"That was your first kiss?" he asked, shocked.

I shrugged, slid onto the floor, and leaned against the bed. I felt stupid and immature. "Justin, you've known me since I was five. You ever seen any guys around?"

"I just figured . . ."

"Figured what?"

He slouched down next to me on the floor. "You seemed so good at it, I figured you must have done it before."

"Don't mock me," I said.

He touched my hand and ran his finger up my arm and back down again. "Seriously, that kiss made me feel drugged up for the rest of the day," he said.

It might have been a better rush than baseball. I touched his face, and he pulled me closer. This time, I kissed him first, and he kissed me back. Then Justin said, "So if I tell Tommy you're my girlfriend now, that would be okay?"

"Yeah, that's okay with me."

We sat there together until it grew dark outside and my bedside lamp gave the room a soft yellow glow. We talked a little bit, but mostly we just sat there, wrapping our fingers together and kissing quietly. Eventually, I heard footsteps on the stairs, and we quickly widened the gap between us.

Brian knocked and stuck his head in. "Hey, Taylor, it's like 10:30. Maybe Justin should go home. It's getting late," he said in his best Dad imitation. Justin stood up.

"I'll walk you out," I said.

Brian made a funny face at me as I followed Justin out of my room. As we descended the stairs, Brian loudly blurted out, "Oh, I get it. You guys are like girlfriend-boyfriend now?"

God, he was such a jerk. Justin laughed and opened the front door.

"Bye, Brian," he said, starting down the sidewalk. "See you later, T."

"Bye, sweetie!" Brian yelled, cracking himself up. I gave Brian a good whack in the arm, but I was in such a good mood, I laughed too.

So now, I was done with Justin. Well, not *done*, but fixed. Fixed baseball, fixed Stacy, fixed Justin. One thing left.

Later that night, I was lying in bed, unable to sleep. I pulled on my sweatshirt and wandered downstairs. I heard the TV on in the family room, and I saw the back of Brian's head on the couch. I stood quietly for a minute, making sure the girlfriend wasn't around. I didn't see her, so I took a step closer. What was he watching? It looked like a home video. Brian still didn't know I was behind him. I continued to watch the TV screen. It looked like our backyard. People were waving at the camera, and Dad was standing by the grill. Wow, he looked a lot younger then. And then I saw her—my mother.

"Is that Mom?" I blurted out.

Brian's head whipped around. "Jesus, Taylor! You scared the crap out of me. How long've you been standing there?"

"Just a second," I answered. "So is it?"

"Is it what?"

"Mom?" I said softly.

He nodded. "Yeah. I think it was like my seventh birthday. I found it in the basement. Weird, huh?"

I sat down and stared at the TV, mesmerized by her. She was handing Brian presents and clapping as he unwrapped them. I saw myself, sitting in a little plastic chair. I was probably two or three at the time. The video was so jumpy, it made me dizzy to watch after a while.

"You remember her, Bri?" I asked.

"Sure."

"You miss her?"

He shrugged. "Not any more. It's been like nine years."

"I don't remember her," I said.

"Hey, you were only five or something," he said.

"Did Dad ever tell you why she left or where she went?" I asked.

"I'm not sure," he said. "A year or so after she left, I found a letter postmarked from France, but I don't know . . ." He paused and scratched his head. "I guess you're old enough now to know why she left."

"You know?"

"Yeah, but Dad doesn't know I know."

I waited and then said, "Well?"

"Well, I read that letter. I guess I was ten or so when I found it. I was snooping around Dad's desk. I don't know why he kept it. It was from Mom, saying she was sorry, but she was in love with Robert and planning to marry him."

"She was cheating on Dad?"

Brian nodded. "It sounded like it had been going on for a long time."

I thought about what Brian had just said. I wasn't angry or surprised, really. I figured Mom was with someone else by now. And I didn't really know her anyway, so it wasn't that big a deal. I felt bad for Brian, though, because he seemed bugged by it. It also explained why Dad hated when I played ball. I reminded him of her, and he probably hated her for cheating on him.

I looked at Brian and said, "Bri, do you ever feel like Dad doesn't like me?"

He laughed. "Are you kidding? I know he likes you. *I'm* the one he hates."

I was shocked. "What? You're his favorite. He went to all your baseball games, coached your team . . ."

"Yeah, but I didn't like playing, so I quit, and he's been pissed ever since."

"He never said that," I said.

"But I know that's what he's thinking."

"Don't assume that. I think he's really proud of you."

"Maybe," Brian said and shrugged. "You should get to bed."

"OK." I got up and headed for the stairs.

"And remember, this stuff about Mom is just between you and me."

"I won't say a thing. Night, Bri," I said.

"Night, T."

CHAPTER 19

Dad came home the following day. The doctor had told him to "take it easy," but I wasn't sure if Dad knew how to do that. He was used to rushing around all the time and working late every night. I was worried he wouldn't be able to rest.

Brian set Dad up on the couch in the living room. He pulled the coffee table next to the couch and placed the remote and a glass of water on the table. Dad lay down, propped himself up on a few pillows, and flicked on the TV.

"Okay, Pop, you're all set," Brian said. "You need anything before I take off?"

Dad shook his head. "No, Bri, you get back to school. Thanks for watching the kids."

"No problem," Brian said, placing the phone on the coffee table. "If you need anything, call me."

"Sure thing," said Dad. "Get going."

Brian gave him a side hug and headed toward me in the kitchen. "You're in charge, Taylor," he whispered. "Call me if you need me." I sat at the kitchen table and stared at the back of my father's head for a while. I wasn't sure what to do, being in charge and all. I went to the cabinet, pulled out some crackers, cut up some cheese, and placed the cheese and crackers on a plate, which I carried quietly into the family room and put on the table next to the water. Dad's eyes were open, and he smiled. "Thanks, sweetheart," he said.

There it was again—*sweetheart*. Maybe the concussion had affected his brain, and he suddenly thought he liked me. Having switched channels, he was now watching the ball game—Yankees vs. Red Sox. I turned to leave, but then thought, *What the heck*, and sat down at the end of the couch, next to his feet. It was a Yankees–Red Sox game, after all.

"What's the score?" I asked.

"Two to one Yanks," he answered. "Eighth inning."

The batter at the plate swung and missed. "Ooh, nice curveball," I said without thinking. My dad looked impressed.

"Listen to you, Miss Baseball. *Nice curve*," he said and laughed.

I perked up. "Well, it was," I said.

"Okay, smarty. Let's see if you can tell me the next pitch."

"All right." I stared at the screen. "Heater," I said proudly. "Too high, though."

"I agree," he said, then was quiet for a while. "How's your fastball these days?"

I was shocked. My father had just asked me about my pitching. I wasn't sure what to say.

"Well?" he asked, waiting.

"It needs more heat, actually, but my coach says my curve is a killer."

And that's how it happened. For the first time in years, my father began to talk to me. We sat there watching the game and talking about baseball. I told him about tryouts and my shutout. He told me about the first time he'd ever gone to Yankee Stadium for a game. It didn't matter to me what we were talking about, though. It just mattered that we were talking. In my fourteen years on earth, it was probably the best day of my life.

After the game ended, he shut off the TV and pulled himself up to a sitting position on the couch. He looked very serious and nervous.

"Taylor, I think I owe you an apology for the last few years."

I was so afraid of ruining a good day, I said, "Dad, you don't have to—"

"Yes, yes I do," he said, waving a hand at me. "The other night after the barbecue, you tried to talk to me, and I brushed you off. I've been a pretty crappy father, and I want to explain. So just let me do this, okay?"

I nodded. "Okay, go ahead." I felt like I was Sacamore for a minute.

He rubbed his eyes and sighed deeply. "You know that picture of your mother? The one you found in my closet?"

"Uh-huh," I answered.

"Well, that's how we met. She was playing on the softball team in school, and I was on the baseball team. Back then, even a girl who played as well as your mom wouldn't try to play with the boys. She'd probably be really proud of you if she knew what you were doing," he said, smiling at me.

I felt a heavy weight on my chest, and I had to hold back the tears.

"In any case, I guess every time I look at you, I see your mother. You walk like her. When you're upset or angry with me, you make the same faces. And you definitely throw a baseball like she did." He laughed. "Except, it seems like you throw twice as fast as she did. Anyway, when I was lying in that hospital bed all alone, all I could think about was that I might die without ever making things right with you."

Now I was crying. Dad shifted on the couch and repositioned his broken arm. "I guess I just thought if I could make you into one of those girlie type daughters who liked to wear dresses and paint her fingernails, it would erase some of your mother from my life. But, the funny thing is, you found baseball yourself, even though I tried to keep you away from it. Or maybe baseball found you."

I wiped my eyes and sniffed. "Yeah, it did. Even though I tried to ignore it, it always came up somehow." I thought about how being angry with my dad had caused me to throw bricks through the school windows, which, in a strange turn of events, led to my winning a spot on the team.

"Dad, I think I should come clean with you about playing on the team this year."

"What do you mean?"

"Well, I don't know if Mom would exactly be proud of me. You see, I was forced to try out for the team by Mr. Sacamore, the guidance counselor."

"I thought you started talking to him after you made the team, when you got into that fight," he said, squinting.

I shook my head. "Actually, I started sessions with him after I, uh, sort of got drunk and threw some bricks through the school windows," I said. I hung my head and bit my lower lip, waiting for him to yell.

"Whoa," he said, surprised. "I guess I really *have had* my head in the sand."

I couldn't believe he didn't yell. "Dad, how many of those pain killers did you take?"

"Lucky for you, probably one too many."

We both smiled at each other.

Then Dad said, "Maybe, after I heal up, I should talk to Mr. Sacamore with you. I never knew you were doing things like that. I can't have my little girl drinking. You know that's a bad choice, right?"

"I do now," I said. *Boy, do I ever.*

"Is there anything else I missed that I should know about?"

"Um, well, Justin is kind of my boyfriend now," I said shyly.

He shook his head. "Okay, that's enough talking for one day. In my fragile condition, I don't think I can handle the thought of you and boys." He pulled the blanket over his head, pretending to faint.

"Dad," I said, nudging him, "are you okay?"

He pulled the blanket back down and smiled. "I guess I'll survive."

Just then, Danny came bounding through the back door. Dad winked at me. "Why don't you go order a pizza?" he said.

"How about Chinese instead?" I suggested.

"Sounds good to me," he said.

Later that night, I headed upstairs to my room. Everyone in the house had gone to sleep long ago, but I stayed up watching late night television because I couldn't sleep. When I got to my room, I noticed something on my pillow—an envelope that said "Taylor." I sat down on the bed and opened it slowly. Inside was a letter written by my father. The faded date in the corner was from four years ago.

The letter read:

Dear Taylor,

If this letter looks faded, it's only because I waited until I felt you were old enough to understand. If at any time over the years, you've felt that I didn't love you, I want you to know that was not my intention. I've been hurt very deeply, and it's been hard to put on a happy face.

I want you to know that your mother did not leave <u>you</u>. She left <u>me</u>. She left me because I was cold and distant, and I didn't give her the love she needed or deserved. She found someone else to love her, and then she left me to start a new life with him. I don't want you to blame your mother for this. It was all my fault.

Your mother left because I wasn't a good husband. And I probably haven't been a great father, either. I feel guilty for driving her away and for the fact that you've had to grow up without a mother. Just know that, although I may not always show it, I love you, and I'm proud of you, no matter what.

Love,
Dad

I read the letter's last line over and over. I sat on my bed and held the paper against my chest and cried. But this time, I didn't cry for me. I cried for my dad. All these years, I'd thought I'd been the only one who was suffering. But when I realized what Dad had been dealing with, I cried for what he'd gone through.

When morning came, I hurried down to the kitchen. Dad was sitting at the table having coffee. Danny was next to him, eating his cereal. I walked over and kissed the top of Dad's head. Danny gave me a strange look. "I've got a game to get to," I said, grabbing a banana. "See you guys later."

"Good luck!" they both said in unison.

When I got to the field and started warming up with Louis, I didn't feel nervous at all. I thought about all the people who cared about me: Justin, my two brothers, my dad, and even Sacamore. I felt like I could take on anything. People really did matter after all.

The whole team was in the outfield warming up, stretching and throwing balls around. I put down my glove and leaned down to tie my shoelaces, when a ball came whizzing by my head at top speed. I looked around to see Rick holding his arms up in innocence. Louis stood up from his catcher's position, took off his mask, and stared at Rick. He walked over and nudged Tony, who'd seen the whole episode. They approached Rick, and about six of the other players fell in step behind them.

I stood frozen and watched. I looked toward the dugout and noticed that Coach Perez was walking toward the outfield to see what was going on, but then he stopped.

Just then, Louis yelled, "Hey, Bratton, what's your problem, man?"

"You trying to hurt our best pitcher?" Tony added,

Rick said nothing.

All the guys started yelling at him, and Tony gave Rick a shove in the shoulder. "You need to check yourself," Tony said.

Coach Perez picked up his pace. When he reached the mob, he pointed at Bratton and said, "I think you need to sit this one out, Bratton."

Rick was shocked. "What?" he said.

"Yeah, I need team players out here, not immature selfish brats. Take your stuff and hit the showers. You're done for the day," he said, pointing his finger toward the school.

All the guys were still crowding around Rick. He knew he'd lost this time. Shaking his head, he jogged away. "Whatever. Good luck without me, losers," he said and kicked at one of the extra balls on the ground.

Louis jogged back toward me as if nothing had happened. He crouched down and slammed his hand in his glove a few times. "Okay, Dresden, let's see some of them curveballs."

With Rick gone, I felt as if a great weight had lifted from me. I relaxed and felt like I was eight years old again.

As I jogged out to the mound for the first inning, I heard a loud cheer come up from the home-side bleachers. I looked up to see Justin, Mr. Sacamore, Danny, and about ten girls from the softball team clapping and whistling.

And sitting next to all of them was my father, looking proud and smiling.

For the first time ever, I could hear him mouthing the words: "That's my daughter."

◇ ◇ ◇ ◇

And so I've come almost to the end of my freshman year in high school—both the worst and best year of my life. I've learned a lot of things about people—and *from* people.

Justin taught me to see the good in everyone.

Trudy showed me how to laugh at myself, and at her.

Mr. Sacamore made me realize that all of us are just trying to figure out how to get through this life with a little bit of happiness.

Even Stacy and Rick taught me something. They showed me that all problems can't be resolved quickly and easily—I still

have things to work out with the two of them, and I will try my best with them.

The person I may have learned the most from is my father. He made me aware that anyone can make a mistake, at any point in life, and that it's never too late to make things right again, especially with family.

As for me, I taught myself a simple lesson—the game of life is hard, but that's also what makes it great.

ACKNOWLEDGEMENTS

I would to thank everyone at Bancroft Press, especially, Bruce Bortz, for making the dream of getting published a reality; Ronda Lindsay, for sticking with me through many drafts; Carolyn Der, for her editing; Harrison Demchick, for writing the screenplay adaptation of the book; and Tammy Grimes, for creating a wonderful cover.

I want to thank my parents, Phyllis and Chuck Griffiths, for always being there through the good and the bad days.

Thank you to my husband, Jamie, for providing me the love that every writer deserves.

I want to thank my three brothers, Michael, Bryan, and Dan Griffiths, for their support and for giving me no choice but to enjoy watching baseball.

I wish to thank my fellow teaching sisters, Amy Gilsenan and Rita Griffiths, for keeping the love of literature alive in their classrooms.

Thank you to Sheila, Jim, and Anne Marie Moesch for your many kind words over the years.

Thank you to all the students of South Orange Middle School, both past and present, for inspiring many of the characters in this book and for letting me share a part of your teen years.

Thank you, too, to all the teachers, librarians, and faculty members at South Orange Middle School for making teaching a pleasure, especially Kathleen Hester, Daniel Savarese, Rebecca Donahue, Susan Wilson, Jane Rauen, and Kathleen Andersen.

And thank you to all the teachers at Vineland High School for teaching me a few things, especially Jeanne Doremus, Peter Starzan, and Kathleen Kopreski.

ABOUT THE AUTHOR

Sara Griffiths, a native of New Jersey, is a seventh grade teacher of language arts in South Orange, NJ. As a teacher at the South Orange Middle School, she's been active in developing a language arts curriculum and producing the school's musical.

A graduate of Rutgers College, where she majored in psychology, she obtained her teaching certificate in language arts from the College of Saint Elizabeth.

Sara is also a certified NARHA (North American Riding for the Handicapped) therapeutic horse-back riding instructor and has seen the physical and mental benefits of involving children in sports.

. She is a member of the New Jersey Education Association, the Society of Children's Book Writers and Illustrators, and the National Council of Teachers of English.

Thrown a Curve is her first published YA novel. She's working on a sequel.

Sara currently lives in White Station, NJ with her husband Jamie and son Ben.